A Bitter Pill to Swallow

The Willowbrook Series

Book 3

By Laura Landon

© Copyright 2023 by Laura Landon
Text by Laura Landon
Cover by Dar Albert

Dragonblade Publishing, Inc. is an imprint of Kathryn Le Veque Novels, Inc.
P.O. Box 23
Moreno Valley, CA 92556
ceo@dragonbladepublishing.com

Produced in the United States of America

First Edition July 2023
Print Edition

Reproduction of any kind except where it pertains to short quotes in relation to advertising or promotion is strictly prohibited.

All Rights Reserved.

The characters and events portrayed in this book are fictitious. Any similarity to real persons, living or dead, is purely coincidental and not intended by the author.

ARE YOU SIGNED UP FOR DRAGONBLADE'S BLOG?

You'll get the latest news and information on exclusive giveaways, exclusive excerpts, coming releases, sales, free books, cover reveals and more.

Check out our complete list of authors, too!

No spam, no junk. That's a promise!

Sign Up Here

www.dragonbladepublishing.com

Dearest Reader;

Thank you for your support of a small press. At Dragonblade Publishing, we strive to bring you the highest quality Historical Romance from some of the best authors in the business. Without your support, there is no 'us', so we sincerely hope you adore these stories and find some new favorite authors along the way.

Happy Reading!

CEO, Dragonblade Publishing

Additional Dragonblade books by Author Laura Landon

The Willowbrook Series
A Willowbrook Miracle (Book 1)
A Page Turner Bookshop (Book 2)
A Bitter Pill to Swallow (Book 3)

Men of Valor Series
A Love For All Time (Book 1)
A Love That Knows No Bounds (Book 2)
A Love That's Worth The Risk (Book 3)
A Love That Heals the Heart (Book 4)

Chapter One

Jenny Dawson left the Claypools' pleasant cottage and took several steps away from the modest home of Mary and Ralph Claypool before she stopped to lean against the rough bark of a large oak tree. She should be elated. Mary had just been delivered of a strong, healthy baby boy, her fifth son to join his four sisters.

Jenny wasn't worried at all about the nine children Mary had birthed in the last twelve years. She was worried about Mary. This last babe had been hard on her. How could a ninth babe not be? What troubled Jenny most, though, was the fact that Mary was young enough she might easily conceive even more children.

It wasn't that she wasn't a good mother. She was an excellent mother. Her children were well cared for, always fed and kept clean, and most importantly, they were all well loved. No, their physical well-being wasn't in question. It was Mary who captured Jenny's concern. The birthing process did not worry her as much as the constant work and care required afterward. Taking care of nine children was simply too much for her to manage. The young woman was working herself to death. Feeding and clothing that many children was more than one person should have to handle. Jenny only wished there was something she could do to ease her burden. Something to make life easier for the woman. But there wasn't. And she wasn't sure Mary would accept help. She loved being a mother. It was all she'd ever wanted out of life.

Jenny pushed herself away from the tree when she heard footsteps approach from behind her. She turned to find herself facing Ralph Claypool.

"Congratulations, Mr. Claypool. Mary has given you another healthy son."

"Thank you, Miss Jenny. But it's not the babe I'm most worried about but Mary. How is she?"

Jenny didn't have a reply for Mary's husband for several moments. She was too surprised at his words to say anything.

Ralph clenched his sweat-stained hat at his waist and twisted it anxiously. "I love my Mary," he said in a thick voice. "More than you will ever know. I'd give up anything to make her happy, including my own life. But I know I'm killing her."

Jenny couldn't prevent a frown from deepening across her forehead. "Why do you think that?"

"It's the babes. I'm giving her too many babes to care for."

"Has Mary told you that?"

He laughed. "No. She wants the babes as much as I do. Perhaps even more. She wants as many babes as I can give her, but you and I know that they are more than she can care for without working herself to death."

"Perhaps you can find someone to help her out," Jenny suggested.

"I've thought of that," he said. "But neither Jenny nor I have any family around what can help us, and I can't afford to pay anyone to come in. I barely earn enough to put food on the table. I'd take on a second job if I could, but working two jobs would only take me away from the house more every day, and that would take me away from caring for the children so Mary has a few minutes to herself." Mary's husband swiped at the wetness that streamed down his cheeks.

"Perhaps you could try to refrain from making love to Jenny. Or, well, there are other methods you could try to keep her from getting pregnant."

"Do you think I haven't tried?" he said, slapping his hat against his thigh. "I'm not the one startin' the lovemakin' most of the time. It's Jenny. And if I tell her I'm too tired, she thinks I don't love her. All I have to do is look at her and I get another babe on her."

Jenny almost wanted to laugh. If it wasn't so tragic, she would have. "Perhaps I can help a little," she said.

"Anything, Miss Jenny. Tell me what to do."

"There's nothing *you* can do. Next time I stop by to see Jenny, I'll tell her she's not healing as quickly as I'd like, and she can't resume lovemaking for at least three months."

"Can you make it four?"

"I can try, but I'm not sure she'll believe me."

"Then I'll tell her you talked to me, too, and instructed me we couldn't couple again until the first of July."

"Do you think she'll go along with your edict?"

"Maybe not, but I'll tell her you were real firm and you'll be angry with me if I don't follow your orders. She likes you too much to go against what you say."

"Well, it's worth a try," Jenny said, patting Ralph on the arm.

"I can't lose her, Miss Jenny. I couldn't live without her."

"You aren't going to lose her, Ralph. Mary's going to be just fine. We'll see that she is."

"Oh, thank you, Miss Jenny. I can't tell you how thankful I am for your help."

"Now, you go in and meet that new son of yours. He's a fine, healthy babe."

"Thank you, Miss Jenny," he said, then turned to the house.

"*Papa! Papa!*" she heard the children call out in excited voices. "Come see what Mama had! She gave us another brother!"

"She did!" Ralph called out in an equally excited voice. "What do you think we should name him?"

"Homer!" the first little voice said.

"Jasper!" a second voice said.

"Linus!" another voice added.

"Peter!" yet another voice cried out.

"We can't call him Peter," the fifth voice called out. "We already have a Peter. That's what we called our last baby."

"Oh, yeah."

"Maybe we should let Mama name this baby," Ralph said. "Since she had him, I think she should get to name him."

"Yeah," a tiny voice said. "Mama will pick out a real good name. She always has the best ideas."

"Yes, she does," Ralph said. "Now, all of you be really quiet and we'll go in to see Mama and the baby."

The voices quieted, and Jenny leaned back against the tree trunk and smiled. There wasn't a better family for a child to be a part of. Love abounded. If only she knew someone who could step in to help Mary and Ralph.

Jenny pushed herself away from the tree trunk and walked along the path to her own small cottage in the middle of the forest. The cottage had been her grandmother's home. Jenny and her mother had lived with her grandmother until both older women died seven years ago of typhoid. Now the cottage was Jenny's. And she lived here all alone.

She opened the door and stepped inside. There was nothing she loved more than the scents that welcomed her when she first entered. The smell of lilac and lavender, and a myriad of other herbs and roots Jenny had boiled or ground to make powders and serums for the potions she used in her medicines. Feverfew that she ground and added to a tea to reduce a fever. The poppy seeds that she ground to make an elixir to reduce pain. There was something for every ailment that plagued someone with an ache or a malady. Thankfully, her grandmother had written the recipes in the book she kept in a place of honor in the cottage. That book was her bible, and had a special cure for seemingly every sickness known to man.

Jenny walked to her worktable and started putting away the jars and bottles she'd taken out before she'd rushed to help Mary birth her babe. She smiled when she remembered the healthy baby. She wished all the babes she delivered would be born that easily, and be as healthy and robust as Mary's. But that wasn't always the case.

Just last week she'd helped birth a babe that only lived four hours before it died in its mother's arms. If Jenny could learn one thing, it would be how to keep more babes alive, and more mothers from dying during the birthing process.

She finished putting away the jars and bottles, then sat down with her grandmother's book of roots and herbs in her hands. She missed her grandmother's knowledge and advice. Although Jenny knew a great deal, she wasn't nearly as proficient as her grandmother had been in knowing what mixtures worked best for each sickness or disease. There were too many things beyond her knowing. Too many things her mother and grandmother hadn't taught her.

Jenny studied her grandmother's book until the sun set and she could no longer see well enough to read, then went to bed. She wanted to rise early and check on Mary and her baby, although she assumed everything would be all right. She could at least sit and hold the infant for a little while and pretend that he was her own. But that would never be.

No one had ever been interested in her. Some even referred to her as a witch. Thankfully, no one had ever been hostile toward her, nor had she ever feared for her life. It wasn't until someone she was trying to help died that the cruel words and accusations came out. Only then did people's true colors show, and she found out what some of the citizens of Willowbrook really thought of her.

Jenny readied for bed and stared at the moonlight streaming through her window. She loved it here—loved the sounds and smells of the woods, and she loved the town of Willowbrook. Thanks to the financial help of the Duke of Willowbrook and his grandson, the Earl of Murdock, the town was growing by leaps and bounds. More businesses were opening every day, and according to the latest gossip, a new doctor had come to town and opened a practice several weeks ago.

Jenny wondered what he was like. If he was as young as some said, did that make him a complete novice? Was he someone she could work with? Or one of those physicians who didn't consider a healer who worked with herbs anyone to be taken seriously. Perhaps, someday, she would meet him. Or perhaps it would be best if she didn't. Perhaps they would be enemies from the start. Jenny hoped not.

A while later, she closed her eyes and fell asleep. She tried not to think about the new doctor in town, but he consumed her thoughts and invaded her dreams.

She knew it was only a matter of time before she met him. Then she'd find out if she liked him or not.

Chapter Two

Dr. James Edwards peeked his head around the door that opened into the patients' waiting room and breathed a sigh of relief. There was only one more patient waiting to see him. One more and he would be done for the day.

It had been a very long day, and he was ready to finish. James knew not to complain about being busy. He'd heard of doctors who had set up practice in a new town and gone days without seeing a single patient. He should be thankful that the people of Willowbrook had accepted him from the start, that he'd had a steady stream of patients.

Of course, the fact that he'd successfully cared for the Earl of Murdock helped. His first patient had been the grandson of the Duke of Willowbrook. The town had been named after the duke who founded Willowbrook. His grandson had been shot, and James had saved him. From that moment on, the people of the town thought he was a miracle worker.

James was glad he had come here. He had been fortunate to see the advertisement for the position of village physician. One of his classmates had pointed the advertisement out to him, and he'd answered the notice immediately. He had been hired the day after he arrived and set up his practice the following day.

This wasn't exactly what he'd planned for his future. He had finished at the top of his class and been awarded several honors and medals of commendation. He had been highly recommended by his professors for a position on the new surgical wing his professor and mentor, Dr. Corman Buchannan, was building onto St. Thomas's Hospital. He had even been sought after by several nationally acclaimed physicians.

But sharing honors with another doctor, and riding on the coattails of a well-known surgeon, was not how he wanted to start his career. He wanted to direct his own future, manage his own practice, and earn a reputation all on his own. And he would settle for nothing less.

James had always known exactly what he wanted. He had always aimed high, both in his professional life and his personal life. His goal was to be the most well-known, most excellent doctor in England, and he had been well on his way to achieving everything he'd wanted. Until…

Adelaide Buchannan, his mentor's daughter, had—to say the very least—complicated his life.

For some reason he couldn't explain, she had attached herself to him and made the assumption he wanted to marry her. She decided the two of them would wed, and her life would be a continuation of the one her mother and father enjoyed. If only that life had been to his liking. But it wasn't. Adelaide Buchannan was the last person on earth he could imagine himself shackled to.

Even though Adelaide's father was an acclaimed physician and had been James's instructor and mentor, James couldn't fathom himself married to the man's daughter. He wasn't ready to get married yet. He had other goals to achieve, other milestones to reach. And none of them included Adelaide Buchannan.

James admitted the last patient and listened to his complaints. The remedy for the illness was simple, and he gave the fellow a tonic and sent him on his way, then closed up his practice for the day. But before he could leave, the door flew open and a well-dressed young man rushed in.

"Oh, Dr. Edwards. I'm so glad I caught you before you left. I need you to check on my mother."

James finished putting on his coat and fastening the buttons. "What seems to be wrong with your mother?"

"She sent a boy to tell me that she's dying."

James stopped buttoning his coat. "She thinks she's dying?" he said in alarm.

"Yes, but I know she's not."

"How do you know she's not?"

"Because she sends someone to tell me she's dying all the time."

"And you don't take her seriously?"

"Of course not. I'm sure there's nothing wrong with her."

The young man might be certain, but James wasn't. "Perhaps we should go check on your mother, just to be certain."

"Yes. That's why I came. I would like you to talk to her and tell her that there is nothing wrong with her."

"Yes. Well, first I would like to see her, just to be sure."

"Of course, Dr. Edwards."

"And you are?"

"Weaver. Orville Weaver."

"It's nice to meet you, Mr. Weaver," James said as he walked out the door. "If you will lead the way to your mother?" he said, then followed Weaver from his office.

The well-dressed fellow led the way to his mother's large, fashionable cottage on the outskirts of Willowbrook and opened the door without knocking when they reached it.

James entered the lovely cottage and stopped short. Mr. Weaver's mother wasn't alone. There was a young female kneeling beside the comfortable-looking rocking chair the woman who was no doubt Weaver's mother sat in. The female turned to face James, and his breath caught in his throat. He found himself looking at the most beautiful woman he had ever seen.

Her hair was quite a unique shade of dark auburn. It glistened in the firelight, and several strands shone with a golden glow. Her face was heart-shaped, and her eyes were large and round and so dark a brown as to be almost black. The moment her gaze locked with his, her eyes sparkled with a life that captured James's attention and refused to let him turn away from her.

"Dr. Edwards," Weaver said, pulling his gaze away from the young female to the older lady. "Allow me to introduce my mother, Mildred Weaver."

"Mrs. Weaver," James said, reaching for the woman's hand.

"Are you the new doctor that came to town a few weeks ago?"

"Yes, ma'am. I am."

"Did Orville ask you to stop and check on me?"

"He was worried about you. You said you weren't feeling well."

"Well, thanks for coming, but I don't need you anymore. Jenny fixed me all up."

"She did?"

"Yes, she knows the right medicine to give me. It works every time."

James reached for the bottle of medicine on a small table beside Mrs. Weaver's chair and held it to his nose. The minute the aroma reached his nose, he raised his eyebrows and put the cork back into the bottle.

"It smells horrible, but Jenny says that's what makes it work so quick."

"I see," James said, then turned to face the woman they called Jenny.

"Have you two met?" Mr. Weaver asked.

"No, I haven't had the pleasure."

"Jenny Dawson, this is Dr. James Edwards. Dr. Edwards, this is Jenny Dawson, Willowbrook's… uh…"

"I am an herbalist, Dr. Edwards," Jenny said. "I use herbs and natural ingredients to cure illnesses. I am also the local midwife. Between my grandmother, my mother, and myself, we have delivered most of the people in Willowbrook and their children and grandchildren."

James nodded in greeting. "It's a pleasure to meet you, Miss Dawson. I've heard remarkable things about you and have been looking forward to meeting you."

"Thank you, but I am sure what you've heard is not so much remarkable as it is simply accurate. There is much to be said for the benefits of herbs and their healing powers."

"Yes," the doctor agreed. "Just as there is for the benefits of modern medicine. Many advancements have been made recently." A look passed between them that James wasn't sure he understood. "Where did you learn your skills, Miss Dawson?"

"From my grandmother, then my mother. Their knowledge was passed down from generation to generation."

"And you chose to follow in their footsteps?"

"Miss Jenny has served the people of Willowbrook well, the same as her mother and grandmother before her did," Mrs. Weaver interrupted. "Her mother was a very good herbalist, but I do think Jenny has her grandmother's gift." Mrs. Weaver smiled lovingly at the young woman.

"I'm sure she has," James agreed politely, "but if you don't mind, I'd like to see what problems brought Miss Dawson to see you."

"My sickness is gone, Dr. Edwards. I don't need you to ask me any more questions."

James opened his bag and removed his stethoscope. When he had situated the ear tips, he took a step toward Mrs. Weaver.

"No!" Mrs. Weaver yelled, holding up her hands to stop him from coming any nearer. "What do you have there?"

"This?" he asked, holding up the stethoscope.

"Yes, what is that?"

"Have you never seen one of these before?"

"No. What is that?"

"It's called a stethoscope. It allows me to listen to your heart. And your stomach. Would you like to listen to your heart?"

Mrs. Weaver looked at the female still sitting at her feet. "Have you ever seen one of those before, Jenny?"

Jenny shook her head. "I've never seen one, but I've heard of them."

James put the ends back in his ears and pressed the stethoscope to Mrs. Weaver's chest. "Would you like to hear your heartbeat?"

Mrs. Weaver looked at Jenny to get permission. Jenny nodded her approval.

James put the ends in Mrs. Weaver's ears, then pressed the stethoscope to her chest.

"Oh!" she yelped.

"Did you hear your heart?"

"Was that my heart?"

"Yes. That was your heart."

"Is that what it's supposed to sound like?"

"That is exactly what it is supposed to sound like. It was beating nice and strong and steady." James turned his gaze to Jenny. "Would you like to listen?"

"Oh, yes," she answered.

James took the instrument from Mrs. Weaver and placed the ends in Miss Dawson's ears. His fingers touched her cheeks, and thousands of electric currents shot through his fingers and up his arms. James's momentary confusion turned swiftly to wonder. Nothing like that had ever happened to him before. And from the shocked expression on Miss Dawson's face, it had never happened to her, either.

He pulled his hands away from hers and lifted the other end of the stethoscope. "Now, press this against Mrs. Weaver's chest and listen."

She did, and her eyes opened wide as a smile lit her face. "That is amazing."

Without hesitation, she turned from Mrs. Weaver to him and pressed the stethoscope to his chest.

"Amazing!" she said with excitement.

James turned. "Now, press the stethoscope against my back, and I'm going to take a deep breath." He did.

"What is that?"

"That's the sound of air going through my lungs. My lungs are clear, but people who come to you with a cold will sound raspy and congested."

She removed the stethoscope from her ears and stared at it as if it were a foreign object. "Astonishing," she said.

"Yes, it is. And this is just one of the inventions that help us determine how ill a patient is."

James studied Miss Dawson's expression. She was truly impressed with his stethoscope. He could tell she was curious about it and eager to learn more. "So, what did you determine was wrong with Mrs. Weaver?"

Jenny reached for Mrs. Weaver's hand and held it. "Mrs. Weaver has a recurring ailment that bothers her occasionally. To ease her condition, I have made up a potion that gives her rapid relief."

"And it works remarkably well," Mrs. Weaver chimed in. "I feel better almost immediately after I take it."

"I can see that you do," he said.

Jenny lowered her gaze to the carpet, and her cheeks turned a deeper red.

"Well, if your ailment has gone away, I think I'll be on my way," James said.

"I'm sorry I brought you out for nothing, Dr. Edwards," Orville said, reaching into his pocket and handing him a coin.

"Nonsense," James replied. "I enjoyed meeting your mother, and it gave me the opportunity to meet Miss Dawson. I have heard so much about her, and finally got to meet her."

He turned to leave, then paused beside Jenny. "Will you be leaving now, as well?"

"Yes, if Mrs. Weaver is ready to retire."

"I am, Jenny," Mrs. Weaver said. "Orville will sit with me for a bit, won't you, Orville?"

"Of course, Mama."

"Then we'll leave you," James said. "And I'll walk Miss Dawson home."

"I'll stop by to see you in the morning, Millie," Miss Dawson said, and they walked out of the cottage together.

"I can see myself home," she said when they were alone.

"No, I'll walk you home. It will give me a chance to get to know you better."

"I'm not sure I want you to know me better."

James stopped, then started walking again when she didn't stop. "I know what you did," he said. "I'm just not sure what you added to the whiskey you put in the mixture you gave Mrs. Weaver."

"An elixir of honey and valerian root."

James couldn't help but chuckle. "No wonder Mrs. Weaver slurred her words and nodded off twice while we were there."

James kept up with Jenny as she increased her pace. It was obvious that she wanted to get home as soon as she could. It was also obvious that she wanted to get away from him.

"Why?"

"Why, what?"

"Why did you give her a placebo? A fake potion?"

"I didn't. That's the potion she needs for what's wrong with her."

"What have you determined is wrong with her?"

"Nothing."

"Nothing?"

"That's right. Nothing. The only thing that is wrong with Millie is loneliness. Her husband died several years ago, and she was left to raise her son by herself. It was just the two of them until Orville married three years ago. Their marriage is a love match, and the girl Orville married likes to keep her husband on a short leash. Millie went from doting on Orville to not having him around her at all."

"So, to get him to pay attention to her," James said, "she feigns an illness, so he's forced to come see her."

Jenny's face lit with a big smile. "And it works. He runs whenever he thinks his mother is ill, and he might even spend the night with her—but when he returns home, he's consumed with his wife, especially now that she's expecting a baby."

"I see," James said on a sigh. "It's too bad Mrs. Weaver didn't have more children. Then her attention would not concentrate on just one person."

"Yes," Jenny agreed, then stopped short.

"What?" he asked when she didn't continue her thought.

"Nothing. I just had an idea that might work." She looked up at him, and her face took on a glow. "My cottage is just down this path. You don't have to come any further. I can make it home by myself."

"Are you sure?"

"Yes, I'm sure. It was a pleasure to meet you, Dr. Edwards. Good night," she said, then was gone.

James watched her leave. She intrigued him. Her understanding of people was remarkable, but her lack of medical knowledge was something that could cause her to miss a hidden problem. And that problem could kill a patient.

CHAPTER THREE

J ENNY ROSE NOT long after midnight. She had slept very little, mostly because her mind refused to erase the picture of Dr. Edwards as he studied Millie Weaver to search for a reason she'd called for a doctor.

Doctors weren't supposed to be so good looking. They weren't supposed to be so young and handsome and cause her heart to stutter when he touched her. They were supposed to be short, and old, with gray hair and a pot belly. They were not supposed to be tall and muscular, with a physique as perfect as the statue of a naked David she'd seen in an art book.

She'd closed her eyes and tried to fall asleep, but after several hours she realized it was useless. She wasn't going to go to sleep, so she might as well get up and make herself a cup of tea, then read another recipe in her grandmother's remedy book.

If only her mother and her grandmother hadn't died when she was so young. If only they had lived long enough to teach her everything they knew about healing. Instead, they had died from the fever that went through the area when Jenny was just seventeen.

Jenny slipped on a robe, then went to the kitchen and made a pot of tea. She sat at the kitchen table while her water heated and opened her grandmother's book to the recipe she had been reading earlier, but found she couldn't concentrate. Her mind shifted back to the thought she'd had when she was walking home from Millie Weaver's.

She fixed her tea then sat back down at the table and smiled. She couldn't know if her idea would or would not work until she tried it, and there was no better time to try it than tomorrow. Nothing was lost if it didn't work, but everything was gained if it did.

Jenny read for a little while until she finished her tea, then returned to her bed to attempt to finally go to sleep. She would need at least a few hours' rest if she intended to implement her plan tomorrow.

※

A FEW HOURS later Jenny rose and dressed for the day. When she was ready to leave the house, she selected the few supplies she might need and went to see Millie Weaver. Her housekeeper showed her in to the breakfast room when she arrived.

"Good morning, Jenny. Have you eaten yet this morning?"

"Good morning, Millie. Yes, thank you, but I wouldn't mind a cup of tea."

Millie's housekeeper brought over a cup and saucer and poured Jenny a cup of tea.

"How are you feeling, Millie?" she asked.

"Much better than last night. Orville stayed with me nearly all night. We had a wonderful talk. He remembered events from his childhood I didn't think were important enough that he would remember."

Jenny smiled. "It's amazing what we remember from our childhoods."

"What's one thing you remember from your youth, Jenny?"

Jenny thought for a moment then smiled. "My grandmama made the best pies in the world, and she made a fresh pie nearly every day. Some of them were for Mama and me, and some of them were to be given away to patients who had been ill and either she or Mama had treated.

"Whenever she made a fresh pie, she would always give me a little lump of dough to make my own pie with. I didn't always make a pie—most often I would just roll the dough out and put butter and cinnamon on it, then roll it up and cut it like she did when she made cinnamon rolls, and she would bake it for me."

Millie smiled at Jenny's story.

"My pies aren't nearly as good as hers were, but every time I bake a pie, I still set aside a little hunk of dough and make my little rolls and bake them."

"That's a good memory," Millie said with a smile. "But that's not what you stopped in for, is it, Jenny?"

"No, not really. After last night I just thought it might be good for you to get out of the house and go for a stroll. Since I had a short call to make, I wondered if you might like to walk with me?"

"Where do you have to go?"

"Just to Ralph and Mary Claypool's."

"Has she had her baby yet?"

"Yes. Just the other day. Another little boy."

"I don't know how she does it. All those babies and so close in age. And they are so well behaved."

"Yes, they are, aren't they?"

"Yes," Millie answered. "I'd love to go see the new baby. It looks like a beautiful day. Perfect for a walk."

"Yes, it is," Jenny agreed.

She waited while Millie retrieved her bonnet and a light coat, and they set off for the Claypool cottage. When they arrived, one of the older children opened the door.

"Oh, Jenny," Mary greeted her from behind her daughter. "Come in. Come in." She looked behind Jenny and saw Millie enter. "Oh, Mrs. Weaver. Come in, please. Follow me. We will go to the sitting room."

Mary led them to a side room that looked as if it wasn't used by the family, but only kept for company.

"Charlotte," she said. "Mind the older children. I'll keep Tammy, Joey, and the baby with me."

"Yes, Mama," answered a child who didn't look any older than eight or nine.

Mary closed the door, then turned to her guests. "Would you care for tea?" she asked, clutching her baby.

"No, thank you, Mary," Jenny answered. "Mrs. Weaver and I just had a cup. Please, sit down. I only came by to check on the babe. How is he doing?"

Mary's face lit with motherly love. "Oh, wonderful. I think he's the most content of all my children."

"May I hold him?" Millie asked. "It's been forever since I've held a baby."

"Of course," Mary said, then placed the baby in Millie's welcoming arms.

"Oh, isn't he sweet?" Millie said in a hushed tone. "My Orville says I'll have my own grandchild in a few months."

"Oh, is your daughter-in-law expecting?"

"Yes. Orville says there should be a little Weaver by Christmas."

"How exciting," Mary added. "Two of my little ones were Christmas babies. Their arrivals were such wonderful events."

Jenny lifted the smallest babe on her lap and leaned back against the cushion. Mary sat with the four-year-old beside her on the sofa, and the three women visited for the next several minutes.

"I can't remember the last time I sat this long without a babe in my arms," Mary said, then laughed. "And look. You have the magic touch with babies, Mrs. Weaver. I think my little Henry was asleep the minute you put him in your arms."

"I always had that effect with Orville when he was a babe. He was asleep minutes after I had him in my arms."

"Then please, come to visit anytime. I'll let you work your magic as often as you want."

Mary paused, then clamped her hand over her mouth. "Oh my. How forward of me. I wasn't asking for your help, Mrs. Weaver. I just…"

"Don't worry, Mrs. Crawford," Millie said on a laugh. "I didn't take it as such, but I wouldn't blame you if you did need some help every once in a while. I don't know how you manage to get everything done and still spend time with your children."

"I do worry about that," Mary said on a sigh. "By the time I get the baking and the cooking done for meals, I feel like I've ignored the children."

"I can see where you would," Millie said. "Perhaps I could call on you every once in a while, and visit with the children, or take them outside on nice days, and you could spend time in your house alone to get things done. Or perhaps just sit with your feet up for an hour or so?"

"Oh, I couldn't impose on you like that," Mary said.

"It wouldn't be an imposition. What else do I have to do except ramble around in that big house of mine all day long?" Millie turned to look at Jenny. "What do you think, Jenny?"

"I think that's a wonderful idea. It would give you something to do with your days and help Mary out at the same time."

"It's settled, then. I will see you tomorrow."

"Oh my," Mary said with misty eyes. "I will look forward to seeing you."

"Well, Jenny," Millie said. "Are you ready to journey back home?"

"Yes," Jenny said with a heart overflowing with happiness. "I have several things to do yet today, and I'm sure Mary does, as well."

Millie reluctantly handed the baby back, and she and Jenny bade Mary goodbye.

"You don't think Mary thought I was being forward, do you?" Millie said as they walked home.

"Not at all. I'm sure she will appreciate the time to herself—and having another adult to talk to. I imagine it's difficult to speak only to children all day long."

"Yes, I suppose it would be," Millie replied on a laugh. She looked at Jenny and smiled. "I can't wait for tomorrow," she said, and Jenny noticed she walked the rest of the way home with a lighter step.

>>><<<

JAMES COULDN'T ERASE Jenny Dawson from his mind. It wasn't only her looks that fascinated him, but her caring manner for her patients. He saw how she interacted with Millie Weaver. She intrinsically understood that there was nothing physically wrong with the woman. Her only ailment was that she was lonely.

James wondered how long he would have examined Mrs. Weaver before he concluded that there was nothing physically wrong with her. He wondered how many pills he would have given her before he realized none of them worked. Yet Jenny had assessed Millie's problem without administering one pill or tonic, except a thimbleful of whiskey and home-brewed valerian root.

James forced himself to forget her ability. That had no doubt been a lucky guess from the beginning. She couldn't have known for sure that loneliness was Millie Weaver's only problem. What if her attacks were only a warning sign of something more serious? What if there really was something wrong with Millie Weaver and he had overlooked it because he'd relied on Jenny Dawson's uninformed diagnosis?

After all, how much training or education had she had? Had she even taken one class in the biological makeup of the human body? Of course she hadn't. And why? Because women were not allowed into medical schools. Women were not allowed to become doctors. They didn't have the ability or the intelligence to become doctors.

James chastised himself. He had allowed a female with a pretty face and an inviting smile to trick him into forgetting his years of study and experience and consider her equal to him in skill and ability. What a fool he had been. He would alter his opinion of her this very moment, and make sure he never allowed her to infiltrate his thinking again. He could never allow himself to believe she was qualified to be a physician.

James stepped out of his office and glanced toward the next patient waiting to see him. This patient was a young man who was doubled over in extreme pain.

James almost had to carry him to one of the examining rooms. Within a few minutes, he determined that young man suffered from an inflamed appendix.

James knew that time was of the essence. Only once had he observed an appendix that had burst, and that patient had died. Once infection entered the patient's bloodstream, it was impossible for them to survive.

James quickly explained what he had to do, then prepared the young man for the procedure. He wasn't sure how he was going to accomplish this operation on his own, but the only person in the office with him was his elderly helper, Mrs. Copper, who served as his receptionist.

Jenny Dawson came to mind as the most qualified person to assist him, but he didn't want to send for her. Asking her to help him would give her the impression that he considered her qualified to be a doctor. Which he didn't. But who else was there? And he needed someone to help him.

"Mrs. Copper," he said, rushing out to the reception room. "Do you know where Jenny Dawson lives?"

"Yes, Dr. Edwards."

"Send someone to fetch her. And tell them to hurry."

"Yes, Dr. Edwards," she answered, and rushed from the office.

James returned to the room where the young man was lying. The first act he performed was to scrub everything down with soapy water, including the boy himself. He had observed that patients who had been disinfected had a much better survival rate than those that hadn't been washed down.

Next, he retrieved a vial of ether and anesthetized the young man. James watched carefully as the boy relaxed, grateful to see he was free of the pain he'd been suffering.

As he was finishing, the door opened and Jenny Dawson rushed in.

"Would you assist me, Miss Dawson?"

"Of course," she answered, then went to the sink by the window and washed her hands with soap and water.

"What do we have here?" she asked when she stepped to the table where the young man lay.

"An appendicitis," James answered.

"Will you be able to operate in time?"

"We'll know soon enough," he answered, then picked up his surgical knife and made an incision.

Chapter Four

Jenny had never seen the removal of an appendix. In fact, she had only seen a handful of surgeries in her life, and those were mainly cesarean deliveries her mother and grandmother were forced to perform when there was a difficult birth and there was a chance they might lose the mother or the baby, or both.

Jenny had only performed a few in all the births where she'd assisted. This would be a totally different experience for her.

"Have you ever seen an appendix removed?" Dr. Edwards asked when he had the patient opened.

"No."

"Your main job will be to keep as much blood soaked up as you can. And watch him so he doesn't wake up. We have to keep him sedated."

Jenny took several lengths of fine cotton and soaked up the blood that was streaming from the incision, then applied more ether to a cloth and held it to the patient's nose when he stirred.

She tried to observe as much as she could while Dr. Edwards worked, but she was so busy with her own tasks that she didn't have time to catch everything he did. Before she realized it, he had removed the appendix and was preparing to close the surgical wound.

He helped her clean as much of the blood as possible, then threaded a needle and began sewing the patient's flesh together.

His stitches were neat and precise, and he worked quickly and efficiently. It didn't take him long, and when he was done, he removed his blood-soaked apron and dropped it in a hamper.

"Thank you," he said.

"You're welcome," Jenny replied. "Will he be all right?"

"He'll survive, if that's what you're asking. Unless he develops a fever. That is often more serious than the disease."

Jenny nodded. She knew that from the patients she had tended.

"Would you care for a cup of tea?" he asked.

"That would be lovely. Shall I prepare it?"

"No, Mrs. Copper will no doubt have some made. She's a tea drinker herself. Will you join me in my study?"

"No, thank you," Jenny answered. "I'll stay with our patient. He should be waking soon. I don't want him to wake alone and not remember where he is."

"Thank you," Dr. Edwards said. "I'd like to have a moment to myself."

"Of course. Take your time. I'll be fine."

Jenny watched Dr. Edwards open the door and leave the room. When he was gone, she relived how magnificently he had removed the appendix. How solid and steady his hands were as he held his surgical knife. How exact and precise his stitches were.

She wondered what someone of his talent and abilities was doing in Willowbrook. It was obvious that he was destined for greater endeavors. Soon he would be known as one of the best surgeons of his time. He would no doubt run one of the large hospitals in London and be known the world over.

Jenny wet a cloth and wiped their patient's face, then placed the cool cloth on his forehead. She wanted to make sure he didn't develop a fever. While she was still caring for the young man, the door opened and Dr. Edwards returned to the room. He carried a cup and saucer in each hand. He set her tea on the table beside the bed.

"I could have come for that," she said.

"I didn't mind. I wanted to come to thank you for assisting me. It made what could have been a difficult procedure much easier."

"I'm glad you thought to send for me. I found it remarkably interesting. Please, don't hesitate to call on me anytime I can be of service."

He looked at her and smiled, and Jenny's heart sped in her breast. He was without a doubt the most handsome man she had ever met. He had no right to be so handsome.

"What brought you to Willowbrook?" she asked when he had relaxed in a chair.

He smiled. "Why? Don't you think I fit in your quaint country village?"

Jenny shook her head. "No. You are obviously destined for much greater things."

Dr. Edwards laughed. "Such as?"

"Such as working in London. Being a world-renowned surgeon. Inventing and improving procedures that will save lives."

"Oh," he said, laughing even louder. It was the most infectious laugh she had ever heard. "You make my abilities sound so lofty."

"They are," she answered. "You are a very gifted surgeon."

"I have known I have a gift for surgery since the day I operated on my first patient. The day will come when I will consider my options, and weigh where my talents can best be used. Until then, I will use my abilities to heal patients like this young man."

He took a sip of the tea that was no doubt turning tepid. "But let me ask you a question. Purely hypothetical, of course. Let's assume I take my talents to London to practice medicine there and am brought a patient just like this one. I operate on him and save his life, which means I am not here to save this young man's life. What will happen to this young man?"

Jenny understood his point. "He will probably die."

"Ah, yes. He will probably die. But in the future, this young man would have grown up, married, and produced three fine sons who would have joined Her Majesty's army and led their soldiers to victory in battle. Because of their outstanding leadership, thousands of lives were saved, and numerous battles won.

"On the other hand, the young man I saved in London turned out to be a gambler and a wastrel. He died in a duel when he was only five and twenty and left his father with a large debt that put his father in debtor's prison. But I received a plethora of accolades because of my skills on the operating table. I became one of the most awarded members of the medical community and received more accolades than I could count."

Dr. Edwards looked at her with a questioning expression. "Where were my talents best served?"

Jenny had no answer for him. "We can't see into the future, Dr. Edwards. No matter how hard we try, it is futile."

"Before I came here, I thought I knew. I thought I knew exactly what I wanted to do with my life."

"What was that?"

"I was going to come to some remote, insignificant village in England and make a name for myself. Then I intended to return to London when my reputation was beyond reproach and join the best medical staff in London."

"Is that still your plan?"

"I'm not sure," he answered. "I find that I like it here. I like what I am doing, and more than that, I enjoy the people and the Village of Willowbrook. I feel that I can do a great deal of good for people in the country who are overlooked and ignored."

"Do you know how special you are?"

"I know exactly how special I am, and I find myself quite lacking."

Jenny laughed. "You are far from lacking, Dr. Edwards."

The doctor finished the tea in his cup and rose to his feet. "Call me when our patient wakes. I think I heard the door open. That means I have another patient to see."

"I will," Jenny replied, and watched James leave the room.

When she was alone, she checked their patient and was relieved to find he was a little warm, but not overly so. Before she could reach for the glass of laudanum-laced wine on the bedside table, the young man opened his eyes and stared at her.

"What happened to me?"

"The doctor operated on you. You had an appendicitis."

"What's that?"

"It is an infection in your stomach. But Dr. Edwards took it out. Just lie still so you don't tear your stitches open and start bleeding."

Jenny held the glass of wine to his lips, and he took a drink. "Not too much. Just a little," she said.

When he'd taken a small sip, she took the glass away from him and went to find James. A few seconds later, he came into the room.

"How do you feel?" Dr. Edwards rested a hand on his patient's forehead, then lifted the sheet and checked his incision.

"Better than I did when I came in," the patient said.

James smiled. "I'm glad. You were indeed hurting. That was obvious."

"I was," the young man said. "I've never had anything hurt so bad in my life."

"I imagine you haven't. Did Miss Dawson give you something to drink?"

"Yes. Some wine with something in it. Whatever it is, it's making me tired."

"You'll appreciate that in a few minutes. Can I get you anything?"

"No."

"Do your parents live nearby?" Jenny asked the young man.

"Yes."

"Would you like us to contact them?"

"Would you?"

"Of course. What are their names?" Jenny wrote down the information the young man gave. "What is your name?" she asked.

"Ted. Ted Black."

"You go back to sleep now, Ted, and I'll send someone to contact your parents."

"Thank you," Ted slurred, then closed his eyes. It didn't take him long at all to fall asleep.

Jenny waited a few seconds to make sure the young man was resting peacefully, then left the room. James followed her.

"Thanks for thinking to contact his parents," he said. "They will definitely want to know what happened to him. And he will need someplace to go when he's well enough to be moved."

"Yes. I can help Mrs. Copper watch him. We will take turns, but I'll have to go home at least once a day. I've herbs to gather and potions to mix. I have several customers who need their tonics."

"Of course."

"Before you go home, why don't you and Mrs. Copper go to the restaurant and get something to eat?" Dr. Edwards handed her money to pay for the food. "I doubt you've eaten all day. Then bring me something back with you. I haven't eaten either."

"Anything in particular?"

"No. Whatever sounds good. And bring our patient some broth. No solids. Just liquids."

Jenny nodded, then went to get Mrs. Copper. They found a young lad and paid him to find Ted Black's parents, then went to the restaurant to eat.

Jenny couldn't describe her feelings. She had never been so impressed with anything or anyone as much as she'd been impressed with Dr. Edwards as he successfully operated on young Ted. It was evident that he was an excellent doctor and an exceptional surgeon. He was too good to waste his time and his talents in the small town of Willowbrook. He needed to be in London. He needed to go where his talents would be used to the fullest. Eventually, he would realize that, and leave.

She was consumed by an emotion she couldn't completely understand. She warned herself that it was foolish of her to become attached to a doctor she had just met, while at the same time, she felt a connection to him that she had never felt to anyone in her life.

She didn't expect him to stay here his entire life, and she knew when he left, he would leave a hole in her life that would be difficult to fill. A part of her dreaded the day he would go on to greater things, while another part of her wanted him to leave before the aching loss she would feel when he left was too painful to bear.

Chapter Five

Several days passed, and Ted Black healed more from his surgery every day. To Jenny, working so closely with James every day was torturous. Every time their hands touched, or he asked her to perform the slightest task to assist him and their gazes locked, spikes of electric currents raced through her body.

The attraction she felt to him was agonizing. How could it be so all-consuming? How could what she felt for him bring such euphoria, yet be so painful?

She tried to keep her emotions hidden as much as possible. She tried not to let him see how much he affected her, but she knew she failed in her attempts.

"How is Ted doing?" he asked her as she left their patient's room after checking on him.

"I think he's almost well enough to go home," Jenny answered, stepping to the other side of the room.

"Is his mother here today?"

"Not yet, but Ted said she would be coming. She had something she had to do at home before she could leave."

"Let me know when she arrives. I want to speak with her. I want you to explain to her what she'll have to do to take care of her son every day, and I need to tell her what she'll need to look for to avoid his wound becoming infected. They will also need a wagon with several blankets to take him home in. The last thing we want is for him to tear open his stitches on the ride home."

Jenny nodded as she wrote down all of the doctor's instructions.

"Can you think of anything else we'll need to tell her?" he asked.

"Perhaps what foods to avoid until he heals more."

"Of course. I should have thought of that."

Jenny lifted her head, and her gaze locked with his huge brown eyes. A smile lifted the corners of his mouth, and his eyes glittered with an emotion that caused her blood to warm as it swirled inside her.

Before she realized his intent, he stepped up behind her and looked over her shoulder to read the notes she had written. He stood so close to her that the warmth from his body heated her back. It took every bit of willpower she possessed not to lean back just enough that her back pressed against his chest.

His hands clamped against her arms, holding her steady, pulling her back slightly as if she was connected to him.

"Jenny?" he whispered.

She breathed a heavy sigh. She was about to give in to him, then realized what they were doing. She pulled away. "I... uh... think... uh... Ted's mother... is here."

"Is she?" he asked.

"I'll go check," Jenny said, then went to the front room to check. Thankfully, by some stroke of luck, Ted's mother *was* just arriving.

"Mrs. Black," she greeted Ted's mother as the woman entered the office. "I'll let you go in to visit with Ted in a moment, but first Dr. Edwards would like to speak with you."

"Is anything wrong?"

"No, quite the opposite. Dr. Edwards thinks Ted will be ready to go home in a day or two."

A smile lit the woman's face. "Oh, thank the Lord. It will be so good to have him home with us."

"I know what you mean. And it will be much more convenient."

"Yes, that it will. I have to call on the neighbors to watch my little ones whenever I come to see Ted. That is why I can't spend as much time with him as I'd like."

"Well, in just a few days, you can spend all day every day checking in on him."

"Oh, yes," she said, dabbing her eyes.

"If you'll follow me, I'll take you in to speak with Dr. Edwards."

Jenny led the way back into the room to see James. She wasn't sure what her reaction would be when she saw him for the first time after they'd had such an explosive encounter. Thankfully, James concentrated on greeting Mrs. Black, and she was spared a repeat of their earlier exchange.

Jenny listened while James explained what Mrs. Black had to do to make sure her son didn't get an infection in his wound, and what foods would be best for him to eat, then they left her with her son. Before she left, he explained that they could come to get him tomorrow afternoon, and to make sure there were several blankets in the wagon to make Ted as comfortable as possible.

Thankfully, there were no more emergencies for the rest of the day. The patients who came in only suffered from minor ailments, and Jenny could avoid being in close proximity with James. She would be glad when she could leave and not have to struggle with his nearness. She had been on tenterhooks for the last several hours.

It was finally the end of the day, and Jenny avoided looking at James as she silently tidied the room that they had used to treat their last patient.

The patient hadn't come in with anything too serious—a cut on his leg that refused to heal. James had treated the wound with a disinfectant, then Jenny sent the patient home with some ground herbs and spices that would help fight the inflammation.

Jenny tried not to think of their reaction to each other earlier in the day, but it was impossible not to relive the heat that had raged through her when he touched her. She wondered if he'd felt the same. But perhaps he hadn't. Perhaps she was the only one who was letting her feelings get ahead of her.

Jenny suddenly realized that her feelings for James were becoming more serious than she could handle. For as much as she enjoyed working alongside him and loved learning what he could teach her, it was quite obvious that she shouldn't be here. She should work from home, where she would not be around him.

Now, all she had to do was come up with an excuse he would believe to leave the surgery.

※

JAMES WATCHED JENNY finish tidying the room they had used for their last patient of the day. "What did you send home with Mr. Charles?"

"Some ground garlic and ginger and a little cinnamon. I told his wife to sprinkle it in some soup and it would help with his inflammation."

He smiled. "That shouldn't hurt him."

Jenny stopped. The expression on her face turned serious. "What do you mean, that shouldn't hurt him?"

"Nothing. I only mean that there isn't anything harmful in the ingredients you sent with him."

"Do you think I would have sent something poisonous with him? That I would intentionally harm someone with my potions?"

"No, Jenny. Of course not. But there is nothing harmful in ginger, garlic, or cinnamon."

"But nor do you think there is anything helpful in the combination."

"I simply don't see how there can be," he answered.

"I see," she said.

"Medicine has made monumental improvements since your grandmother's time."

"And you believe my grandmother's methods no longer serve a purpose?"

"I believe your grandmother's way of doing things has been replaced by newer and better methods that work faster and more efficiently than the older procedures."

James saw the expression on Jenny's face change. Her eyes lost their vibrance. A frown etched across her forehead.

"May I ask you a question?" she said. Her tone of voice was void of the friendliness he had become used to hearing when she spoke.

"Of course."

"You have seen me work with patients for several weeks now, and you have seen several examples of my abilities. What do you think of my ability to become a doctor?"

James felt like he had stepped into a quagmire of quicksand. He knew that the more he fought his way to the surface, the faster he would sink. The wisest course of action would be to give her no answer at all, but he knew that Jenny would not accept that.

He smiled in hopes his expression would soothe the lack of details in his answer. "You are one of the most talented females I have ever seen when it comes to treating patients."

"But not as talented as male physicians," she added.

"You are not supposed to be as talented as male physicians. That is not your job, just as I am not as proficient when it comes to raising and caring for children."

"I see," she said.

"Jenny, don't—"

"No, James. Do not apologize or try to soften your opinion of my abilities. It will only cause you to dig the hole you've got yourself into deeper."

"You are angry," he said. "Please, don't be. I did not mean to say anything to offend you."

"But you meant what you said."

"I was being honest with you. I thought that is what you would appreciate. I realize now that I shouldn't have been quite so…forthright."

"No," she said, grabbing her bonnet and reticule. "You should always be honest with me. It avoids any misunderstanding between us."

"Jenny, please don't be angry."

"It's time for me to go, James. I'll see you tomorrow, unless I have patients who need my *limited* abilities at home."

James watched her turn her back on him and leave the room. The door closed shortly after her.

He slammed his hand against the wall then raked his fingers through his hair. What had he done? Why had he opened his big mouth and said what he had? What a fool he'd been.

He took several long, angry steps across the room and threw the door open. He stepped out into the evening air and locked the surgery door before he turned in the direction of Jenny's cottage. He walked at a rapid pace, wanting to catch up with her before she reached her cottage. He knew if she went inside, she'd lock the door and wouldn't open it no matter how long he knocked.

He watched the path ahead of him and finally saw her in the distance. He called out to her, but she didn't stop. In fact, she walked faster.

"Jenny," he called out again.

She ignored him and walked even faster.

James ran until he caught up with her. Once he reached her, he stepped in front of her to force her to either stop or run into him. "Stop, Jenny," he said, then clasped his hands around her upper arms.

"Let me go," she said.

"No. You'll run if I do."

"What do you expect me to do? Stay here so you can throw more insults at me?"

"I didn't mean to insult you."

That was when he noticed her eyes were damp and tears streamed down her cheeks.

"Just leave me alone," she said again, struggling to free herself from his grasp.

"No," he whispered, unable to lift his eyes from hers. Their gazes locked, and her great brown eyes filled with more tears.

He'd hurt her. Even though he hadn't meant to, he'd insulted her and belittled what she did to help people. James tried to imagine how he would feel if someone did that to him. And he didn't like it.

"I'm sorry, Jenny," he said, pulling her closer to him and wrapping his arms around her. "I'm sorry," he whispered, lowering his gaze to her lips. "I'm sorry," he whispered again, then lowered his head and kissed her.

※

JENNY KNEW WHEN he looked at her lips that he was going to kiss her. A voice in her head told her to push him away, to stop him, but she didn't. She couldn't. And yet she knew kissing him would be the biggest mistake of her life.

She didn't want to know what it felt like to have his arms around her. She didn't want to know what it felt like to press her body against his. She didn't want to know what it felt like to kiss him, because she knew that once he kissed her, she could never survive without his kisses ever again.

When he pressed his mouth to hers, the passion it ignited burst through her body with the force of a bomb exploding on a battlefield. She tried to convince herself his kisses were not so all-consuming, tried to pretend that she could handle their heated exchange without showing how much his insults had affected her. She tried to pretend that his kiss did not affect her, and yet...

...her knees trembled beneath her. She skimmed her hands up his chest and wrapped her arms around his neck. The pace of his breathing began to fall into rhythm with her own as she tilted her head and opened her mouth to grant him entrance. With a welcoming gasp she allowed him to deepen his kiss.

His tongue skimmed her lips, then entered her mouth. Their tongues touched, then battled as if his goal was to conquer. And conquer he did. Sweetly, she gave in to him without a fight.

He kissed her again and again, and didn't stop until they were both exhausted and breathless. Then he lifted his head and wrapped his arms around her in a scintillating grip that saved her from collapsing to the ground.

He held her for several long, satisfying moments.

"That didn't mean what you think it might," she said when she was able to speak. When she was able to breathe. Maybe saying the words out loud would make them believable.

"I shouldn't have kissed you," he whispered.

"No, you shouldn't have," she agreed, even though she would have regretted it forever if he hadn't.

When she was able, she stepped far enough away from him that he couldn't hold her. "I must go home."

"Will I see you tomorrow?"

"No," she said after a moment to think about her answer. "No, not tomorrow."

"Will I see you the next day?"

"I don't know," she answered honestly.

He took a step toward her, but she stepped back, out of his reach.

"I need you, Jenny."

She shook her head. "No you don't. That's the problem. You want me, but you don't need me."

"That's not true. I need you. I couldn't have managed operating on Ted Black without you."

"No. You couldn't have managed operating on Ted without someone, but that someone could have been anyone else. Even Mrs. Copper."

"No," he said, shaking his head.

"Yes, James." She turned her back on him. "Goodbye, James," she said, and left him, perhaps for the last time.

She tried to pretend that giving him up was the wisest move she could make, but she couldn't convince herself that it was. She knew it would be the most difficult. Perhaps impossible. She was falling in love with him. She had already given him a large part of her heart, and the longer she stayed with him, the more of her heart he would possess.

She tried to digest what he had told her, what his opinion of her was. He'd said he needed her, but he didn't. Not really. He wanted her to be with him. To help him. To be his assistant. But anyone would do. Anyone who was capable of doing what she had done to help him operate on Ted Black. That was all he needed. And what he'd made more than plain was that he did not consider her in the same category as him.

She was a female. She could never be a doctor.

She went through the door to her cottage and closed and locked it. She wished she could lock out his words as easily as she had locked him out of her cottage.

Chapter Six

Jenny carried in a small pot of juice she had pressed from the bark of a willow tree and placed it on her table. Willow bark juice was excellent for pain. Her mother and grandmother before her had relied on it to ease headaches, as well as a woman's monthly pain.

On the way across the kitchen, she paused long enough to stir a pot of roots she had boiling over the fire. Then she stopped to lift her kettle of boiling water off the flame and finished steeping her tea.

When her tea was ready, she sat at the table and took a sip with a bite of biscuit she had made earlier in the day. That would be enough for her evening meal, along with some cheese. She wasn't very hungry right now. She hadn't been hungry since she'd told James goodbye and walked away from him more than a week ago.

She would like to say that each day was easier to stay away from him, but that would be a lie. Each day was infinitely harder. She missed him more all the time.

Every afternoon, a little boy would knock at her door, and when she answered, the little tyke would give her a handwritten note. The notes were all the same. They said:

I miss you more today than yesterday.

Please, come back.

Jenny would tell the messenger there was no reply, then reward him with a piece of anise candy she had on hand. This had gone on for more than a week... until today. No one had come today. Maybe James had given up. Maybe there would be no more notes.

A part of her hoped there wouldn't be. She wasn't sure how much longer her heart could stand the pain. But another part of her prayed he would never give up on her. Knowing that she had lost him for ever would hurt infinitely more, even though she knew it would be for the best.

How could she care for someone who considered what she did insignificant? Who considered her love of medicine and of healing simply playing at being a doctor? Who didn't think it was possible for females to be physicians?

Jenny swiped at her eyes to wipe away the tears that threatened to spill down her cheeks. She had shed enough tears over how deeply he had hurt her. She refused to shed any more.

She placed the cloth she had used to wipe her tears on the table, then stopped short when there was a knock on the door.

Her little boy was late tonight. She reached for a piece of anise candy and went to the door.

The minute she opened it, her heart skipped a beat. She had to tip her head back to meet the eyes staring at her. Huge brown eyes. Eyes that had mesmerized her from the first moment she'd looked into them.

"Is that for me?" James asked, pointing to the candy in her hand.

Jenny tried to slam the door in his face, but he wouldn't let her. He reached out and prevented her from shutting it.

"No, Jenny. This has gone on long enough. It's time we settled it."

"There is nothing to settle, Dr. Edwards. You are a doctor who has made a temporary stop in Willowbrook on his way to bigger and better positions in London, and I am nothing more than someone you can look down on and scoff at."

Jenny tried to shut the door again, but when James's foot prevented it from closing, she gave up and turned away from him. She returned to the table and sat down to finish her tea.

He followed her into the cottage and sat across from her.

"Are you going to offer me some tea?" he asked.

"No, you won't be here that long."

Instead of arguing with her, he rose and searched her cupboards until he found a cup, then poured himself some tea from the pot sitting on the table.

"What do you want?" Jenny asked.

James took a sip of his tea, then slowly lowered it to the table. "I want to apologize. I didn't mean to come across like I did. I didn't mean to sound so judgmental."

"That's the problem, James. You *did* mean to sound judgmental. You meant every word you said because that is exactly how you feel. You don't consider what I do as an extension of the medical profession. Nor do you think anything I prescribe is as helpful as what you prescribe."

"That isn't—"

"Stop it, doctor! That is *exactly* what you think."

He didn't answer her because he couldn't. He closed his mouth and kept it closed.

"But I could overlook that. What I cannot overlook, however, is that you consider women so far beneath you in intelligence and ability that it is preposterous for us to think that we can become doctors."

"I didn't say that, Jenny."

"But you thought it. What you thought when you asked me to assist you to operate on Ted Black was obvious. I was capable enough to assist you, but the minute I was so bold as to ask a procedural question, you cut me off. You considered it foolhardy to want to know more, as well as a waste of your time to tell me."

He held her gaze for several silent moments. "It pains me to admit you are correct. It is quite difficult for me to confess it, because I always considered myself to be quite open-minded. Quite forward thinking. But you have shown me that I am not that at all, am I?"

"No, you are not. But I should not have expected you to be. You have never seen a woman doctor, just as I had never seen a male doctor until you arrived."

"And I have been a disappointment to you, haven't I?"

"Not a disappointment. I am in awe of you. I am in awe of your talent and ability. But I am disappointed in how reluctant you are to accept things that are new to you."

"I have much to learn, then, don't I?"

Jenny could not help but smile. "Yes, you do. Your professional knowledge and ability is far and above anything I have ever seen, but your skills with people need improvement."

"Then please come back and work with me. I will teach you everything I know about medicine, and you can teach me how to interact better with people."

Jenny shook her head. "I can't."

"Please, Jenny. I need you."

She lowered her gaze to her hands in her lap. She shouldn't. Every voice in her head shouted that she should stay away from him, but her heart said something different. Something completely different. "I can't, James. It will never work."

"We will make it work. We will both make sure it works."

"How? Our abilities are too far apart."

"Then we will forge them to become closer. You can observe what I do to heal patients, and I will learn what herbs and roots you use to ease a patient's suffering."

Jenny thought for several moments. More than anything, she wanted to learn from him. She wanted to know how to be a better healer. And she wanted to spend as much time around him as possible. She felt whole and complete when she was near him. She wanted to be close to him until he was no longer with her. She didn't want to be away from him until he left her and wouldn't be near her any longer.

"On one condition," she finally answered.

"What's that?"

"That you promise me that you will never kiss me like you did."

"I owe you an apology for that. My forwardness was uncalled for. I should never have allowed myself to get so carried away."

"Is that how it always is when you kiss a female?"

His eyes opened wide, and he stared at her. "No, that's not how it is when I kiss other females. That's only how it is when I kiss you. Is that how it is when you kiss other men?"

Jenny shook her head. "I wouldn't know. I have never kissed anyone before."

James raked his fingers through his hair. "Oh, Jenny. I am so sorry. I had no right to kiss you like that. I got completely carried away. I promise it will never happen again."

"Do you give me your word?"

"If I give you my word, will you come back to help me again?"

She hesitated a few moments. She wasn't sure what she should do, but her heart gave her an answer. She was so miserable without him that she couldn't stay away any longer. And there wasn't a better teacher than James to help her learn what she didn't know.

"All right, James. I will come back, but only to learn from you.

"Are you saying nothing can come from our association except for that of student and teacher?"

"Of course nothing can. Don't you understand? We can't allow anything to develop between us."

"Why?" he asked. "Don't you feel the attraction between us?"

Jenny rose from her chair. "That's the problem, James. I feel a strong attraction growing between us, but that attraction is futile."

"What if it's not?"

"We can't allow it to grow into anything more serious."

"Why, Jenny? What if it is supposed to?"

"It's not. Don't you understand? The day will come when you will tire of the small village of Willowbrook and the limits it puts on you. You will realize that you are destined for greater things. You belong in London, where you can do the most good."

"What if I tell you that I don't ever want to return to London? That London is not where I want to live my life?"

"But you are destined for greatness, James."

"I can achieve greatness wherever I am happiest. Perhaps that is in Willowbrook."

"Is there something in London that you're running from?"

The expression on his face changed. It turned darker.

"London holds no attraction for me, Jenny."

"But Willowbrook does?"

"Yes. Willowbrook does. Now, will you come back to work with me? Will you help me become a better doctor, and allow me to help you learn to be a better doctor?"

She shouldn't allow him to talk her into coming back to the surgery, but she couldn't turn him down. Not only because she was so desperate to learn from him, but because she was so desperate to be around him as much as she could be.

She closed her eyes, hoping to find the strength to refuse his offer, but knowing it was not there. Finally, she nodded her agreement.

He gave her a sharp nod, then a heart-melting smile. "I'll see you in the morning, then," he said, then rose and left her.

As he moved away, his shoulders twitched, shifted, then settled, as if he were throwing off a burden he no longer needed. And Jenny knew she had just made the biggest mistake of her life.

⇶⋘

JENNY WORKED WITH James week after week and learned more than she thought possible. She learned how to set a broken arm and the fastest, neatest way to stitch a cut.

And James learned the best herbs to use to make potions for fevers and infections. Together, they taught each other several methods that improved their skills—Jenny's as a surgeon, and James's as an herbalist. And each week they grew closer together.

One day, Jenny entered the room where James was tending a patient. She watched as he mixed several potions into a small container, then poured a small amount into a jar. "What is this for?" she asked softly.

"I thought I'd mix some ingredients to send with my patient to drink in his tea to help with his fever."

Jenny lifted the last bottle he'd used and read the ingredients. Then she took the bottle to the other side of the room, where she and James couldn't be overheard. "Does your patient have a severe case of constipation?" she whispered.

James shook his head. "No, he has a wound that needs to be watched."

"Well," Jenny said, struggling not to laugh, "if he takes your potion, it won't do much to heal his wound or keep it from getting infected, but it will do wonders for his bowel movements."

James braced his hands on the counter and avoided looking at her. "What do I want to send home with him?"

"A mixture of honey and garlic."

"Yes, that's right. How could I have got that wrong?"

"I don't know. You just weren't concentrating."

"That must have been it," he said on a frustrated chuckle, then went in his patient's room to deliver the poultice. When he returned, he grabbed her and gave her a quick kiss. "Thank you! You saved my career."

"My pleasure," she answered, then left the room before she asked him to kiss her again. She'd missed his kisses, missed the closeness of his body pressed to hers when he kissed her. Most of all, she missed the emotions that raged inside her when he kissed her.

>>><<<

JENNY TRIED TO tell herself that each day James was in Willowbrook was a gift he gave her until he was gone, and the memories she stored up would last her the rest of her life, even though she knew they would not. But she was thankful for each day that went by that he didn't tell her he would be leaving.

At the end of one day, Jenny prepared to leave, and James stopped her.

"Why are you in such a hurry?" he asked.

"I have to collect some roots and berries," she said. "I'm getting terribly low. I usually never let my supply get so depleted."

"Do you mind if I go with you?"

Jenny smiled. "No, not at all. You need to know what you're looking for when you dig them, though."

"Yes," James said with a smile. "I wouldn't want to dig up a weed thinking it was ginger root."

"That's for sure," she said, then headed out the door and down the path that led to her cottage.

"Is this the cottage your mother and grandmother lived in?" he asked.

"And my great-grandmother before them."

"Did she heal with herbs, too?"

"Yes. I don't believe anyone in my family was anything but an herbalist."

"Do you know how amazing that is?"

"I know I'm very fortunate to have all that knowledge written down for me."

"Yes, you are."

They reached the cottage, and Jenny handed James a small tool.

"Follow me," she said, then led him around the side of the cottage. She entered a shed-like structure covered thickly with vines and bark. It was dark inside, the air warm and moist. It felt more like a grotto than a shed.

"My word," James snorted. "It's a bloody greenhouse."

"And root cellar," Jenny beamed. "Plants that won't grow in the wild, I grow here. Ones that like it cool and dry go down there." She pointed to a small pit lined with burlap. "Ones that like it warm go up here." Jenny moved to the left and stepped up on a low platform. James followed.

"It's like a jungle up here," he exclaimed, as sweat began to appear across his forehead. Jenny chuckled and opened a small grate to reveal a bed of coals where a wide flat pan of water simmered. The arrangement kept the pallets on the platform bathed in tropical steam.

She dug up a bulb of ginger and held it out to him. "This is what they look like. Dig carefully," she said. "We only need a few."

It wasn't long before they had a small basket full of ginger root bulbs.

"Now what?" he asked.

"Follow me," she said, and led him out of the greenhouse to a white willow tree. "Do you have that tool I gave you?"

"Yes."

"Willow bark is best for pain relief, but of all the willows, white willow seems to be strongest. Cut two or three strips of bark off the trunk—about eight inches will do—and put them in your basket."

"And this," she said as she bent to caress a delicate white flower, "is feverfew. Never, never be without it! And"—she grinned—"never, ever let it go to waste." She swept up the blossoms nearest to her and arranged them along the side of her basket.

"For fever? These innocent little ladies?" James bent and caught up a small handful of the blossoms.

"Yes! And to induce labor."

"Really?"

Jenny worked hard not to bristle at the young doctor's skeptical tone. "Yes. Really."

"These white ones but not those yellow ones?"

Jenny sat back on her heels. "Well yes, but no! Bring the dandelions as well."

"Now you're having me on." He laughed.

Jenny punched him in the sleeve. "Dandelion fights infection. Bring as many as you see."

James slowly shook his head, clearly struggling to believe. Reluctantly, he did as he was told.

"Now, we need one more item, and this is the one we cannot do without. I have it in the cottage."

"What is it?"

Jenny walked into the cottage and took down a rope of bulbs that hung from a peg near the vegetable bin.

"Garlic?" James said in amazement.

"Yes, garlic. Pound it, then mix it with honey in a cup of tea, and it fights throat and lung infections better than anything we have."

"Do you have any honey?"

Jenny pointed to half a shelf lined with jars of honey. "My bees were quite productive this year."

"I see that," he said, his eyes glinting with admiration. "What are you going to do with these now?"

"I'll let them dry out, then pound them and put them away until we need them."

"I see," James said, looking at everything they had gathered. "That's quite a collection."

"Let's hope we have more than we'll have use for."

"Yes," he said, then headed out the door. Jenny followed him, but before she could walk with him even a few steps, she heard voices calling from behind her cottage.

"Dr. Edwards! Miss Jenny!"

"Dr. Edwards! Miss Jenny! Come quick. Come quick!"

James and Jenny raced around the side of the cottage. The two Wilson boys were waiting nervously for them.

"Come quick!" one of the boys yelled. "You need to get to the Fleischer house as quick as you can."

"What's wrong, Jeb?" Jenny asked, grabbing the boy by the shoulders as she tried to calm him.

"I don't know. It's Mrs. Fleischer. She's real sick and she's burning up. Mr. Fleischer says he's never seen anything like it. He thinks it might be a plague."

Jenny turned her gaze to lock with James's. "I'll go. You go back to the office. Send some men out to tell everyone to stay in their homes until we know what it is."

She turned back to the Wilson boy. "Jeb, run to the Claypool cottage and tell them to stay inside and not leave."

"Is it bad?" Jeb asked.

Jenny knew the Fleischers, knew Mr. Fleischer had been in the wars and was aware more than most how to recognize a dangerous fever.

"I don't know, but we don't want to take any chances, do we?"

"No, ma'am."

"And don't go inside. Did you go inside the Fleischer cottage?"

"No. Mr. Fleischer wouldn't let me. He made me stay in the lane."

"Good. After you tell the Claypools, you go home and get your family inside, and stay there until Dr. Edwards tells you it's safe to come out."

"All right," he replied, and the two boys took off on a run toward the Claypools.

"What, Jenny? What do you think it is?" James asked.

Jenny let her gaze lock with James's. "I don't know, but it could be typhoid fever."

He stared at her wearing a dark look. "Have you ever seen anyone with typhoid?"

Jenny nodded. "That's what my mother and my grandmother died from."

"Did you have typhoid, too?"

"Yes. That's why I will be the one to treat Mrs. Fleischer. I've had typhoid before. I can't get it again."

"Are you sure?"

"Yes, I'm sure," Jenny lied. "I'm going to get a few things I need and go to the Fleischers'. If anyone else comes down with a fever, get them to the Fleischers'. I'll set up a room for them."

James nodded, then grabbed her shoulders. "Stay safe, Jenny."

"You too," she said, then raced back in her cottage to get everything she might need. This was going to be a long night.

A long couple of weeks.

As Jenny gathered the supplies she would need, her thoughts returned to the weeks that the fever had raged through Willowbrook nearly ten years past. When her mother and grandmother suffered so terribly. The days and nights she cared for them. The time she held their hands as their bodies were ravaged by the symptoms of typhoid.

She remembered the hours she held their hands, praying that their sickness would go away, but knowing that it wouldn't. She felt once again the despair that coursed through her when the hands of her loved ones went limp in her own. When they breathed their last.

Jenny didn't want to relive those painful memories, but she knew she was about to.

She put everything she needed into her baskets, hoping it would be enough, and went to the Fleischer cottage. Who knew how long it would be before she could return, or *if* she would return.

Chapter Seven

The minute she entered the Fleischer cottage, her worst fears were realized. Mrs. Fleischer did indeed have typhoid. The symptoms were all there: high fever, headache, nausea, stomach pain, rash on the abdomen and chest, confusion, and hallucinations.

"Has your wife been anywhere lately?" she asked Mr. Fleischer after she got him and his three children settled in the stable.

"Yes, she just returned yesterday from London. Her sister wrote her that she was ailing, and my Connie went to help her until she got better."

"Did she get better?"

He shook his head. "No. She passed. Connie took it hard. She and her sister were close. At first I thought she was ailing 'cause she was taking her sister's death so hard, then I realized this was more. That's when I sent for you."

"I'm glad you did."

"Do you know what she has?" he asked.

"My guess would be typhoid fever."

Mr. Fleischer's face paled. "I remember when the typhoid went through here nearly ten years ago. We lost a lot of people. Your mother and grandmother were among the ones who died, if I remember right."

"Yes." Jenny tried to appear brave, though she felt anything but.

"Did your wife go anywhere after she returned home?"

"No, she was feeling too poorly."

"Did anyone stop by to see her?"

"Only Mrs. Carville. But she didn't stay long after she found out Connie was sick."

Jenny tore off a piece of paper and wrote James a note to check on Mrs. Carville, and if she was running a fever to have her husband bring her to the Fleischers'. Then she placed it on a tree stump where the Wilson boys were to check and relay messages. She was so glad they'd made those arrangements earlier. Then she went back inside the cottage and cared for Mrs. Fleischer.

CONNIE FLEISCHER TOOK a turn for the worse around midnight, and Mrs. Carville arrived around the same time, along with her eight-year-old daughter.

Connie died before sunrise, and before noon the following day, Jenny had three more patients to care for, all of them children. They seemed to be hit the hardest, much harder than adults.

And by noon the next day, Jenny had four more patients to care for. Thankfully, Mrs. Copper from Dr. Edwards's office came to help her. She claimed she had survived the last typhoid infection and was prepared to meet her maker if that was what God wanted, but she wanted to do as much good as she could before she died. Her words brought tears to Jenny's eyes, and she gave Mrs. Copper a big hug and sent her to care for the children who were ailing.

Day after day went by, and each day brought more sickness and disease, until finally, one day went by without a new case of typhoid. Jenny prayed the worst of it was over—but she was proven wrong when the next day a young mother arrived with her infant daughter.

"Don't let my baby die, Miss Jenny," Kathrine Overton said when they brought her and her baby into the Fleischer cottage. They were both suffering from typhoid, and from the advanced stages of the symptoms, they'd had the disease for a long while.

"I'll do my best, Katherine. I remember she was a strong little one when I helped you deliver her."

Jenny saw a slight smile lift the corners of Katherine's parched lips. "Yes. I remember you… saying… you'd never… heard a baby… cry so loud. That meant… she wanted to… come out… and… see… the world."

"Yes. I remember. And you called her Siren."

"Yes. I was sure… the entire… village… heard her."

Jenny rinsed a cloth in water and wiped the perspiration from Katherine's face.

"Don't worry about me…" Katherine said. "Just keep… Siren safe. Don't let her… die. Joe… will take it… hard if… she doesn't… make it."

"You're both going to make it, Katherine. Joe will take it hard if either one of you don't make it. You fight. Do you hear me?"

Katherine didn't answer. She'd lost consciousness.

Jenny took as much care of her and little Siren as she could, but several hours later, before the sun had risen above the horizon, she went to Katherine's bedside to try to force her to drink some water. But it was too late. She was already gone, and so was her baby. Katherine had died with her baby clutched to her breast, and Siren had died safely held in her mother's arms.

Jenny's legs weakened beneath her, and she crumpled to the floor in a heap. She could not stop the tears from spilling from her eyes and streaming down her cheeks.

Just then, she heard a whistle from outside the cottage and knew James was here. There was nothing she wanted more than to rush into the sunshine and wrap her arms around him, but that wasn't possible. She couldn't dare allow him to come into such close contact with so many people with the fever.

She waited until she was sure he was gone, then went out to see what he had left her. She grabbed the bundle of supplies and took it inside.

There were several ingredients she needed to fight fever and pain for the typhoid. And a fresh supply of tea because they were almost out. And some pastries from the restaurant, and homemade breads that the residents of Willowbrook had sent. And, in the bottom of the bundle, there was a folded scrap of paper.

Stay strong, sweetheart.
There's a light at the end of this dark tunnel.
Love,
J

Jenny clutched the note to her breast. If she hadn't been sure if she loved James before, there was no longer any doubt. She loved him with her heart and soul.

SHE BATTLED CASE after case until she could hardly stand on her feet. Another brave woman from Willowbrook came in to assist them, and another, until Jenny and Mrs. Copper finally had two hours of uninterrupted sleep to themselves. Jenny woke feeling like a new person. She hadn't known it was possible to feel so exhausted. But evidently it was.

Another week went by, then a month, until Willowbrook finally saw its last new case of typhoid fever. Jenny cared for the new patients until their fevers broke and their symptoms left. Then she waited the two-week period where they were out of danger of developing any new cases and sent everyone home.

The day when the last patient went home was a joyous time indeed. Jenny collected what was left of the supplies she had brought with her and bade the Fleischer family goodbye, then went to her cottage. She intended to sleep at least a week before opening her eyes again.

The only person she had missed was James. He had usually stopped by at least once or twice a day to deliver bakery pastries or a meal from the restaurant, but she hadn't seen him for the last three days. If he was like her, he'd gone home, lain down to take a nap, and hadn't woken up for the past three days.

She smiled thinking of him getting the sleep she was so desperate to have. She could not wait to get to her bed, but first she was going to have a nice, hot cup of tea and a pastry she'd taken from the Fleischers'.

Her cottage came into view, and she smiled at the sight of it. On second glance, she realized that something wasn't quite right. The door stood open.

Jenny approached the cottage with measured steps, taking care to check for any intruders. She entered the kitchen and looked around. No one was there, nor was anyone in the sitting room. She was going to head to the bedroom next, but before she reached it, she heard a low, agonizing moan. Someone was there, and Jenny was sure she recognized the voice.

The only emotion that surged through her body was an ice-cold rush of panic that flowed through her veins. She placed the supplies she'd carried with her on the nearest table and ran to the bed.

"James!"

She felt his forehead and pulled her hand from his flesh. He was burning up. He was as hot as any of the patients she had treated.

She ran to the sink and pumped the water until it came out cold, then she filled a basin and a pitcher and carried it in to him. After placing a cool cloth on his forehead, she poured water into a glass and made him drink.

"Oh, James. How long have you been sick?" she asked, even though she knew he wasn't alert enough to answer her. "Why didn't you come to see me earlier?"

"Ohh…" he moaned again, then doubled over.

"Yes, James. I know. You're in pain."

She raced to the fireplace and lit the wood chips, then heated some water to make tea. While the water was heating, she mixed some garlic with honey and added it to the tea she brewed. She also had a small amount of white willow bark for him to chew and forced the tea with honey and garlic down him.

In the meantime, she changed the cloths on his forehead with cooler ones, then removed his shirt and placed more cool cloths on his chest.

Over and over, she replaced the cloths on his forehead and chest, then tried to get more tea down him. The only patient she'd treated that was as bad as James seemed to be was Mrs. Fleischer, and she hadn't survived.

Jenny placed more cloths on his heated body and continually told him that it was important that he survived. "You can't give up, James. You have to live. You don't have a choice. I won't allow you to give up," she told him in the fiercest voice she could manage through her tears. She wasn't sure what she would do if she lost him. He was too important to her. Far too important.

The next morning, Mrs. Copper came by with some broth and pastries. "Is Dr. Edwards here?" she asked from outside Jenny's cottage.

"Yes, Mrs. Copper. But he has the fever. Don't come any closer."

With reluctance the woman set the broth and pastries on a bench outside the cottage door and backed up. "I was afraid of that. I searched all over for him and couldn't find him. This is the next place I looked after the Fleischer cottage, and they told me you'd gone home. How is he?"

"Not good. He's as severe as any of the patients we treated."

"Do you need me to come in and help you?"

"No. I need you to stay away so you can bring me supplies when I need them. I'm going to try to get some broth into him. He needs to eat something. I'm not sure how long it's been since he's eaten."

"All right," Mrs. Copper answered. "I'll be back in the morning."

"Thank you," Jenny replied. "Oh, Edith. Thank you for everything you did. It was very brave of you to come into the Fleischer cottage. I don't know what I would have done without you."

"That means the world to me, Miss Jenny. I was glad I could be of use."

"You were more than 'of use,' Edith. You were a lifesaver."

"You try to get some sleep, Miss Jenny. You've got to be wore out from all the patients you tended."

"I am, but I'll be fine. I have to make sure Dr. Edwards survives. How many people did we lose?"

"Rumor has it we lost twelve. Five of them were children."

"Oh."

"They're saying you and Dr. Edwards are heroes. Without your quick actions, we would have lost more than that."

"We have you to thank for that, too, Mrs. Copper."

"We all did what we had to do," Mrs. Copper replied. "Now, you tell the doctor there that I said he is not allowed to die on us. We need him too badly."

"I'll tell him," Jenny said, then watched her only link to the outside world walk away.

She gathered the food Mrs. Copper had brought then poured some broth into a cup and tried to force James to take a bit. But he refused. She did, however, get some tea into him. She rinsed several cloths in the cool water and placed them on his forehead and chest. He was mostly unconscious, rousing infrequently, and that bothered her more than anything else. Until he was well enough to regain consciousness, he was in mortal danger.

She continued to give him anything that would reduce his fever and eliminate his infection. But nothing seemed to work.

<hr />

ONE DAY TURNED into another, then another, and another, yet James did not improve. In fact, Jenny feared he was getting worse. His fever remained high, and perspiration ran down his face in rivulets. She continued to change the cloths on his forehead and chest, but that didn't seem to help. All that helped was prayer. It wasn't that James seemed to get better, but he was still alive. That was a major accomplishment. Jenny gave God the credit for keeping him alive so far.

On the fourth day, or perhaps it was the fifth, Jenny feared even her prayers could no longer help. She entered the room, and instead of hearing James's raspy breathing and pain-filled moans, all was silent.

She rushed to the bed and placed her hand on his forehead, then broke out in tears. His forehead was warm, but it wasn't hot. His cheeks were warm, but they weren't burning. His face was flushed, but it wasn't scarlet.

"James?" she said, rinsing a cloth and wiping his face.

His eyelids fluttered, then opened. He looked at her as if he wasn't sure where he was, or who she was.

Jenny wanted to speak to him. She wanted to hear his voice, but she could not get any words out of her mouth. She was crying too hard. She was too emotional.

"Don't... cry... Jenny," he whispered in a raspy voice.

"I can't... help it... you silly man. You frightened me... half to death."

"I'm... sorry," he finished, then collapsed against the pillow and closed his eyes.

Jenny rushed to the kitchen and poured some tea with honey and garlic into a cup, then prepared some of the broth Mrs. Copper had delivered that morning and took it to him.

"Here," she said, propping up his head. "Drink this." She held the tea to his mouth first, then the broth. Then she gave him more tea. "You have to take as much liquid as you can. You've lost too much fluid."

"How long was I sick?" he asked when he had drunk his tea.

"I'm not sure. I found you four or five days ago. I don't know how long you were here before I found you."

"How many... did we... lose?"

"Twelve, I think."

"That's too many," he said, "but it... could have been... worse."

"Yes, it could have been a lot worse."

"Am I the... last one?"

"Yes, James. You are the last one."

Jenny made herself a cup of tea and sat down in a chair beside James's bed to drink it. It was the first cup of tea she had enjoyed in more than a week.

"Have you... slept at all?"

"Enough," she answered.

"That's the... second lie you've... told me," he slurred.

"What do you mean that's the second lie I told you?"

"You have not got... enough sleep. The circles... under your eyes... are as black... as coal."

Jenny smiled, then laughed at him. "And what's the first lie?"

"That... because you had... typhoid before... you could not get it... again. You could have... died, Jenny."

"But I didn't," she replied. "And, thank God, neither did you. Now, go to sleep so I can take a nap," she whispered, then closed her eyes.

Chapter Eight

James spent most of the next three weeks sleeping. He tried to stay awake when Mrs. Copper came each day to bring pastries from the bakery, and lunch from the restaurant. But mostly he tried to stay awake long enough to hear her news. Her visits were the only opportunity he had to hear what was going on in the outside world.

Everything in Willowbrook was nearly back to normal. Jenny had been called to assist in the birth of Orville Weaver's son. According to Edith Copper, Millie Weaver was over the moon. Now she had two households to visit every day, and another babe to care for.

The best news James received was Jenny's permission for him to get out of bed and walk around outside. She even let him go with her to collect roots and berries and leaves, which he watched her dry then grind to a fine powder. He wasn't sure what all of them were, or what they were used for, but he found that he was quite fascinated with them.

One particularly warm day, she entered the cottage after being out on a call to treat someone with a fever. After their recent scare with typhoid, everyone was extra cautious when it came to fevers. Thankfully, this was nothing more than the onset of some sniffles. Jenny's cure for this type of fever was warm tea with honey and garlic. James was all too familiar with the taste of the tea. He'd had enough of it when he was running a fever.

"I need to dig ginger roots and garlic. Would you like to accompany me?" she asked.

"There's nothing I'd enjoy more. Does this mean you no longer consider me a health risk and I can go back to the office?"

Jenny nodded.

"Does that mean you'll come back to work with me?"

"I'm not sure. Haven't you seen enough of me?" she asked.

"You know I haven't, Jenny. Have you seen enough of me?"

"No, James. I wish I could say I have, but I haven't."

"Good," he said with a smile. "Then let's go dig those ginger roots." And he headed out the door.

***

JENNY WATCHED JAMES as he dug one ginger root after another and dropped them into the pail she'd brought with her. She knew what going back to work with him would mean. She would be in contact with him every day and would grow closer to him every hour she was with him. She feared her emotions were changing and that she was learning to care for him more than was wise—or safe.

She couldn't allow herself to forget that the day would come when he would leave and return to London. He was not meant to spend his life here in the country. He belonged in the city, where he could use his skills to their fullest. He was destined for a greatness he would never achieve here. And if she gave him her heart, he would leave her broken and alone when he left.

The wisest thing she could do was keep her distance from him and avoid having a broken heart, but she had already discovered how impossible it was to stay away from him.

"So," he said, dropping another ginger root into her bucket. "Have you given any more thought into coming back to working with me at the surgery?"

"I will consider it," she answered. "If you give me your word."

"What would you like my word on?"

"That you will not allow our emotions to come between us."

He hesitated a moment. "You have my word," he said.

"Then I will return in the morning."

He smiled at her, and her heart skipped in her breast.

"Thank you," he said. "Now, I have another question for you."

"What?"

"I had a visitor today."

"Who?"

"Orville Weaver."

"Was something wrong?"

"No."

"Was it his mother? Is she ill?"

"No. She is not ill. She has been too busy to be ill."

Jenny smiled sheepishly. "Oh."

"Do you know what she's been doing?"

"Actually, I do. She's been helping Mary Claypool for a few hours every day, then stopping by to see her new grandbaby and taking care of him for a while."

"Whose idea was that?"

"Actually, it was mine. It was obvious she used the excuse of being ill as a way to get her son's attention. Once he married, he had a difficult time finding time for his mother, so when she wanted to see him, she pretended to be ill. I realized she needed something to occupy her time. She mentioned that she'd always wanted a large family but only had Orville, so I took her to meet Mary Claypool. She had just had her ninth child and desperately needed help. When Millie saw all those children, she fell in love and wanted to return to help. I thought it would be a wonderful way to occupy her time and not miss her son too much."

"And your plan worked perfectly. She has spent so much time at the Claypools that she hasn't had to call on her son once."

"Oh, has he missed his mother?"

James laughed. "I believe he has."

"Good," Jenny said with a grin on her face.

"You are quite the schemer, aren't you?"

"I saw the chance to help two women who needed each other, so I made it happen."

"Your idea was brilliant."

"Thank you," Jenny replied. "Do you mind if I ask *you* a question?"

"Of course not. What would you like to know?"

"Do you regret setting up your practice in Willowbrook?"

When he looked at her, his gaze turned more serious. "No, I do not regret coming to Willowbrook. Not at all. In fact, I am glad I came here." He paused. "What about you?"

"Me? How can I regret coming here? I have never been anyplace else."

"No. Do you regret that *I* came here?"

Jenny lowered her gaze and smiled. "No. I don't regret that you came here. In fact, I am very glad you came here. I can't imagine never meeting you."

"And I can't imagine never having met you," he said, then reached for her hand and held it. "Think of all we would have missed out on."

"Yes. We have made several memories to cherish."

"Like going through a typhoid epidemic together."

Jenny laughed. "That will be a memory, for sure. But I am not convinced it will be at the top of the most enjoyable memories."

"Me either," he said with a smile.

They talked several moments more before James got to his feet. "I'd best get back to my surgery and make sure Mrs. Copper hasn't frightened off all my patients."

"I can assure you she has taken excellent care of your surgery."

"I'm sure she has," he said, then turned to leave. "I'll see you in the morning," he said, then walked down the path.

Her heart swelled in her breast, and she was more at peace than she'd been in a long time. For the first time in her life, she knew what it felt like to be in love.

Chapter Nine

The days went by in perfect harmony. Whenever James had a procedure he thought Jenny would benefit from watching, he called her into the room. He was impressed by her seriousness and the intensity with which she watched every move he made. When the procedure ended, she asked a multitude of questions, then wrote his answers down in her notebook.

"By the time we're done, you're going to know as much as I do," he teased her one day after he had a patient with a knife wound he needed to treat. What he didn't expect was her answer when he asked her what she would use to treat the wound.

"I would use a mixture of garlic, cinnamon, and ginger," she said. "What would you use?"

"I would probably use garlic, cinnamon, and ginger."

"You would not," she said on a laugh.

"No. I'd treat it by keeping the wound clean and dry, then using warm compresses."

"But you haven't applied anything that will help heal the wound," she said.

"No, but hopefully it will keep it from getting infected. There are some things that even modern medicine cannot prevent."

"Then perhaps it might be wise to consider falling back on what herbal medicine can do," she said.

He paused as if considering her words. "Perhaps you are correct. I would like to hear more about what your mother and grandmother would have done."

"Would you really? Or are you just saying that?"

"No. I really would. This might be an area where I can learn from you."

"Perhaps it might," she said. "What are you most concerned with?"

James thought for a moment. "Infection. I am most afraid that the wound I just treated will become infected and there will be nothing I can do. What would you put on it?"

"Honey."

James looked at her as if she had grown two heads. "Honey?" he asked.

"Yes. For years, honey has been used as an aid to reduce inflammation and infection. I would mix it with finely ground garlic powder."

"You are serious, aren't you?" he said in disbelief.

"Oh, yes. My mother and grandmother both used honey to prevent infection. And they used garlic for its infection-fighting abilities. These are herbal remedies that have been used for thousands of years."

"Have you ever seen them work?"

"Oh, yes. Quite often."

"Perhaps I should call our patient back after lunch and apply some honey to his wound."

"Would you do that?"

"Of course I would. I would be very interested in evaluating the results. But first, I want to get something to eat. Would you like lunch?" he asked.

"I don't have time today. I need to restock some of my herbs. I am dangerously low."

"I'll come with you, then. I'll pick up lunch for us to eat, then help you gather your herbs, then we can eat."

Jenny smiled, and James couldn't help but match it.

"That sounds perfect. I will be in the forest south of my cottage."

"I'll meet you there after I pick up our lunch."

Jenny put on her wrap and her bonnet, then went out the door.

James finished locking up, then went to the restaurant and ordered dinner for them, as well as a bottle of wine. When he had everything he needed, he walked down the path that led to her cottage.

He headed for the woods to the south of her cottage and found her sitting on the ground, digging up roots and picking flowers.

"You found me," she said when he came near her.

"Of course I did. I always seem to find you."

She laughed, then put more roots into her basket.

"What are you gathering today?"

"Garlic roots and more dandelion. Then I must spend some time in the greenhouse and cultivate more turmeric."

"What do you do with that?"

"An extract of turmeric does wonders with arthritis." Jenny put her tools down. "Are you ready to eat? I am starving."

"So am I," he answered, then took the food out of the basket. James opened the wine while Jenny set out the edibles. When he had poured the wine, they ate.

"This is delicious," she said, eating the fried chicken and sweet potatoes.

"Wait until you see what we have for dessert," he replied.

"What?" She tried to peek in the basket, but James had the lid closed so she couldn't see what was inside. "What is it?" she asked again.

"Just eat your chicken, then you can have your dessert."

JENNY TOOK ANOTHER bite of her chicken as she focused on him. James had prepared a wonderful time to relax and replenish, to sit idly in the shade and shed the day's tensions. Yet she felt anything but relaxed. Jenny felt more alive than she knew a person could feel, just sitting close to this dear man.

No one had the right to be so handsome. No one had the right to be so perfect. It wasn't fair, especially when she had fallen in love with him, and that love was something she could never act upon.

She finished her chicken and sweet potatoes, then put her plate next to the basket.

"Are you ready?" he said, placing his plate on top of hers.

"Yes." Jenny took a swallow of her wine, then placed her glass on the blanket next to the basket.

"Here you go," he said, then placed a thick piece of peach pie in front of her.

"Oh, how did you know? Peach is my favorite!"

"Mine too," he said with a broad grin.

Jenny picked up her fork and took a bite. "Oh my. It's delicious."

"Good," he said before taking a bite himself. "Oh, it is," he said, smacking his lips.

When they had finished their pie, they reclined on the blanket. James lay with his head propped on his crossed arms. "This is perfect," he said, studying the cloudless sky. "A perfect day for a picnic."

Jenny lay on her side with her head propped on her hand. "Mama would send me out to collect roots and leaves and flowers, and I never minded. It was always so peaceful here."

"Do you resent that I came?" he asked.

"Resent that you came? No, why would I?"

"Because from the number of patients I'm fortunate enough to have been able to treat, I imagine you are not as busy as you used to be."

Jenny smiled. "Don't worry about that. I'm still plenty busy. Have you noticed that most of your patients are men?"

A frown creased his forehead. "Now that you mention it, they are."

"Do you know why that is?"

He slowly shook his head.

"Because women often prefer to go to a female when their ailment has to do with female problems or pregnancies."

"I have never thought of that."

"Well, it's just the way it is."

"When do you treat female patients?"

"In the evening, when I return home."

"Oh," James said thoughtfully. "That makes you put in terribly long days, then, doesn't it?"

"I don't mind."

"I think we need to do something to fix that problem," he said.

"I'm fine with it."

"No, I'm sure the women that come to see you don't want to wander through the woods in the dark."

"No, that is a negative when they have to come at night."

"Then we'll make sure they can see you during the day."

Jenny panicked for a moment. She was afraid he was going to tell her she could not work with him any longer, and she didn't know how she would handle that. She so enjoyed watching him work.

"I don't mind seeing the women in the evening."

"You may not, but I have plenty of rooms at the surgery. You can use one of those to see your patients, and I will use another one to see mine."

"Really?"

"Of course. Then I will have an opportunity to meet some of the women who come to you. Of course, I won't interrupt you when you're treating them. That would defeat their purpose of not wanting to see a male physician. And when necessary, you can refer a case to me, and I can refer a case to you."

"Are you sure, James?"

"I am very sure," he said, then shifted his gaze to her lips. She knew he wanted to kiss her, but he wasn't going to. If she wanted him to kiss her—which she did—she would have to ask him to. He had promised her he wouldn't kiss her like he had the last time, and she knew he wouldn't go back on his word.

She reached out her hand and cupped his cheek. "I need you to kiss me, James."

"Are you sure?"

"Oh, yes. I am sure." And she lowered her head and pressed her lips to his.

He raised his arms and wrapped them around her neck, then applied pressure until her lips were melded to his. His kiss was gentle, yet all-consuming. Jenny couldn't deny the passion there. It stirred her unlike anything she had ever experienced.

He deepened his kiss, and Jenny answered his desire with a passion that equaled his.

She had struggled not to, but she knew she had fallen in love with him. She'd told herself he would break her heart, but it was too late. She was already in love with him, and when he walked away from her, he would take pieces of her broken heart with him. But she didn't have a choice. She couldn't do anything except give him her heart and pray she'd survive when he left her.

He kissed her again, then again, then his hands roamed over her body. She knew she should stop him, but she couldn't. She wanted him too badly. She wanted to know what it was like to make love to him and have him make love to her. She wanted to know what loving him was like.

She wanted that one memory to cherish for the rest of her life.

James wrapped her in his arms and rolled her onto her back, then came down over her. His hands caressed her and his body worshiped her.

And he gave her the most perfect experience she had ever had in her life.

Chapter Ten

Neither James nor Jenny mentioned what had happened in the forest that night. James knew he should say something to her, something to reassure her so she didn't think what had happened was insignificant, or that it hadn't meant anything to him. It had meant a great deal.

She had given herself to him without reservation, had given him her virginity, the most valuable gift a woman could give any man. And he loved her for it. He'd known he loved her before they made love, but hadn't realized how deeply and completely. But he knew now. He only wished the opportunity would come up where he could tell her. Unfortunately, every time he attempted to broach the subject, she found a way to stop him from talking about their feelings for each other.

The first time he had attempted it, she'd made an excuse to leave the room. Another time, she had changed the subject, saying she didn't have time to discuss what they'd done.

Her last excuse had stopped him from bringing up the subject again. She'd stopped him with a curt retort and told him that she refused to speak to him about what happened between them because it didn't mean anything. She made it clear that the event that night was so insignificant that it wasn't anything unusual. But how could she expect him to believe that when he'd been the first man she'd ever made love to?

James tidied up after his last patient, then went into the room where Jenny had treated hers. She was still washing things down, as they had decided was necessary after each patient.

"Did you have anything interesting today?" he asked when he entered the room.

"Yes—Mrs. Chavers is going to increase Willowbrook's population sometime early next spring."

"Oh, wonderful. I know they've been anxious to start their family." James sat in an empty chair. "Have you stopped in to check on how Mary Claypool and Millie Weaver are getting along?"

"No, I was going to do that, but time just has a way of getting away from me."

"Then why don't we call on them when we lock up today?"

Jenny's expression changed, and he knew she was trying to come up with an excuse not to go with him.

"There is no reason for you to refuse, Jenny. It's time we checked in on them, and we're going to have to spend time together sooner or later. You can't continue to avoid me forever."

"I'm not avoiding you, James."

"Yes, you are. Every time I bring up the subject, you shut me down."

"I just don't see a point in discussing it."

"You say the word 'it' as if we're talking about a puddle we stepped into and got our boots muddy."

She looked at him, then covered her hand over her mouth to stop herself from laughing.

"What?" he asked.

"I'd hardly compare what happened to a puddle we stepped into."

"Well, what would you call it?"

She lowered her gaze thoughtfully. "A mistake, James. A very large, catastrophic mistake."

"I see," he responded. "Well, I don't."

"How can you not? I never should have forced you to make love to me."

"You didn't force me."

"Of course I did. You would not have gone any further than simply kiss me if I hadn't asked you to."

"You don't know that," he said.

"Yes, I do. And so do you. You gave me your word, and you wouldn't have gone back on it."

Their conversation came to an end when Jenny reached for a shawl and wrapped it around her shoulders. "If we're going to go, we'd better leave before it gets dark," she said, and walked out the door. James led her from the surgery and locked the door after them.

They walked to the Claypool house in silence, but before they reached the cottage, they were greeted by the sound of children's laughter. James looked at Jenny and smiled. "I think Millie Weaver is doing a fine job of entertaining the children."

"It sounds as if she is," Jenny replied, then sped up her steps until she could see the children in the yard playing with a large ball.

"If it isn't Willowbrook's amazing doctors," Mary Claypool said, coming toward them with a baby on her hip. "Isn't this a wonderful sight?"

"Yes, we could hear the laughter before we arrived," Jenny said.

Before she could say anything more, James noticed a man coming toward the children. He stopped to stand beside Millie. Then he clapped several times and started the game they were playing again. He tossed the ball into the circle of children and cheered when one of the smaller ones kicked the ball.

"Who is that man?" Jenny asked Mary.

"That is Ralph's father. He arrived two weeks ago and has been a godsend. The children adore him, and Ralph and I think he has taken a shine to Millie."

"Really?"

"Yes. They seem to spend a great deal of time together."

"Isn't that interesting," Jenny said.

"What are you building?" James asked, indicating a structure attached to the house.

"That is an addition to our cottage," Mary replied. "Ralph's father is building it. He said our cottage is too small for the number of children we have."

"Wise man," James said with a smile.

"I can't wait until it gets finished," Mary said, then took Jenny's arm. "Please, come in. Mrs. Riddles was just taking some pastries out of the oven."

"Who is Mrs. Riddles?" Jenny asked.

"Mrs. Riddles is Millie's cook. Millie spends so much time here that she decided she didn't eat at home enough to warrant Mrs. Riddles staying there, so she brings her every day, and she cooks our meals."

"That's a wonderful idea," Jenny said, looking at James and smiling.

"I'm getting terribly spoiled," Mary said, leading them into the cottage. "I have more time than I have ever had in my life. It's wonderful."

James followed the ladies into the cottage, and Mary introduced them to Mrs. Riddles, then served them pastries and tea.

He couldn't believe how perfectly things had turned out for Ralph and Mary Claypool. And Jenny deserved the credit for everything. All because she'd treated the patient instead of the disease. She realized there was more a doctor could do for his patients than treat them physically. There were often emotional problems that were more important.

This was another lesson he could learn from her.

They had stayed too long at Mary Claypool's, but when Millie and Ralph's father joined them, there was simply too much to talk about to leave. Just as Jenny feared, it was turning dark when she and James walked home.

She wasn't afraid of the dark. In fact, that was her favorite time of the day. But after what had happened the other night, she didn't want to be alone with James in the moonlight. There was something about moonlight that brought out emotions she didn't want to have to deal with. Tonight was no different.

She shivered when she relived the passion they'd shared.

"Are you cold?" he asked, removing his jacket and wrapping it around her shoulders.

"No, I'm fine," she answered, but instead of accepting her reply, he wrapped his arm around her shoulder and held her closer to him.

If she were wise, she would have pulled away from him, but it felt so safe and secure in his arms that she couldn't force herself to step away. They walked together until they reached the path that led to her cottage. "I can walk the rest of the way by myself," she said, stopping to remove his jacket.

"Just keep it," he said, pulling the lapels close beneath her chin. "You can bring it to the office tomorrow."

Jenny lifted her gaze and looked into his eyes. Their gazes locked, and heaven help her, she wanted him to kiss her.

Instead of turning and walking away from him, she skimmed her hands up his chest and wrapped her fingers around his neck, then applied the pressure necessary to press his lips to hers.

The kiss they shared was filled with an emotion that represented the desire they felt for each other. It exemplified the hunger that could not be assuaged. It proved that what they felt for each other was more powerful than Jenny thought it could ever be.

He deepened his kiss, and Jenny accepted his intrusion, then let her tongue battle his. But this time she had the willpower to stop before their affections got out of hand. She pushed herself away from him and walked toward her cottage.

He called after her, but she didn't stop, nor did she slow down. She couldn't. She needed to think. She needed to decide what she must do.

One thing was certain—she couldn't continue to work with him any longer. The day would come when he would decide to return to London. His talents were too great. There was no limit to the heights he could achieve. But he would never reach those heights in Willowbrook. And it was she who would be left behind.

Jenny finally reached her cottage. She opened her door and closed it behind her, then locked it. She wrapped James's jacket around her and sat in the dark. She didn't think he would follow her, but she didn't want him to know she was there if he did.

She needed to think. She needed to decide what was best to do. She couldn't return to the surgery and work with him. She wanted him too much. She was too desperate to be near him. Too desperate to touch him and have him kiss her. That could never happen again. She knew that now.

Tomorrow she would return to the surgery with her handcart and gather all her supplies. When she had everything loaded, she would return his jacket and never see him again. She would work out of her home like she and her mother and grandmother had done for generations. The sooner she returned to life as it had always been, the sooner she could mend her breaking heart.

Chapter Eleven

Jenny rose early to be sure she arrived at the surgery before James. She wanted to have everything packed and ready to take home before he arrived. The less time she had to spend near him, the easier leaving him would be. But when she entered the surgery, he was already there.

He sat in his office with a letter in his hands. He wasn't reading it. It was almost as if he had it memorized and was simply staring at it to make sure it was real.

She decided not to bother him, and walked past his office door and into the room she used to treat her patients. It didn't take him long to appear before her.

"I'm glad you're here," he said from the doorway. The expression on his face was strained and the letter was still in his hands. It hung loosely from his fingers.

"Is anything wrong?" she asked. She knew whatever the letter contained, the news was anything but welcome.

"No," he answered. Then, "Yes. Something *is* wrong, Jenny. I have to leave for London."

"I see."

"I'm not sure how long I will be gone, but I'll leave you in charge until I return."

"Are you sure?"

"Yes, you can still use the surgery. There's no sense in making your patients go all the way to your cottage."

Jenny nodded. She didn't have the courage to say anything more.

"When will you leave?" she finally asked when she found her voice.

"I'm not sure. By the end of the week. Perhaps early next week."

"Oh," she said, not expecting his answer. She'd imagined that he would be in a bigger hurry to leave. "Does your leaving have something to do with the letter you received?" She glanced at the letter dangling from his fingers.

"Yes. It's from one of my professors, Dr. Buchannan. He's the head physician at St. Thomas's Hospital."

"He must be very important, very influential, if he's the head of the hospital."

James nodded. "He is."

Jenny wanted to ask him if the letter mentioned what his professor wanted to talk to him about, but she didn't. She knew if she asked, he would answer her, and if he did, it would feel too final. She would know for sure that his professor intended to offer him a position in London. The position he had always dreamt of having. The position he was meant to have.

Thankfully, there wasn't an opportunity to ask. The outside door opened, and she heard Mrs. Copper speak to their first patient. There was a rush of patients from then on.

It wasn't until they'd treated their last patient of the day that she had the opportunity to speak to James.

"When you came in this morning, I noticed that you had two baskets and a handcart with you," he said. "Did you need them for anything special?"

Jenny was cleaning the room for the next morning and stopped. She couldn't bring herself to tell him that she'd intended to pack her supplies and not return. That was no longer necessary.

"I have some roots and leaves to gather and I… uh… I was going to go out after I was done here."

"So, you carried the two baskets here this morning, just to carry them back home now?"

Jenny pretended that she hadn't heard him. She finished wiping down the table and the equipment she had used.

"Why were you going to leave, Jenny?"

She stopped her movements.

"Why?" he asked again, this time louder and angrier.

"I have to, James. This won't work."

"What won't work? Why won't it?"

"It won't work because I'm falling in love with you." Jenny tried to keep the tears from falling but couldn't. "I'm falling in love with you, and the day will come when you'll leave Willowbrook."

"How do you know that?"

"Because you *can't* stay here. You are destined to do greater things than just be a small-town country doctor. You belong in London, where you can create new and better ways to operate on people. Or invent new medicines to cure diseases."

"But what if I don't want to practice medicine in London?"

"You have to. And I can't continue to work with you until I've fallen so in love with you that I can't live without you, only to have you leave me. My heart isn't strong enough to survive that."

Tears streamed down her cheeks, and she couldn't stop them. Her heart was breaking, and there was no way to mend it. She wrapped her arms around her middle and let the tears fall.

Like a warm blanket that covered her, James took her in his arms and kissed her. "I am not going to leave you, Jenny. I love you too much to leave you."

She shook her head. "You have to leave. I couldn't live with myself if you gave up all your dreams and talents to stay in Willowbrook. You're meant for greater things, not living in the rural part of England

and help me dig roots."

He brought her closer to him then tipped his head back and laughed. "There's nothing I'd rather do than help you dig for roots and tear bark off trees."

"Oh, James," she said through her tears. "Don't you see? I can't let you stay. I can't."

"You can't make me go, either," he whispered, then lowered his head and kissed her with all the pent-up emotion he felt.

She accepted his passion-filled kisses and returned them with a desire that surpassed his. She had never imagined she could love someone as much as she loved him. Never thought it was possible to want someone as much as she wanted him. But she needed him more than she had ever needed anyone. And he wanted and needed her as much.

And he loved her.

He kissed her one final time, then broke the kiss. "We need to dig those roots before it gets too dark."

"Yes," she said, grabbing her shawl and turning to the door. Except she knew gathering roots wasn't the only thing they would be doing beneath the starlit night sky.

⇶⋘

IF JAMES COULD have put off going to London any longer, he would have, but time had run out. He knew his news would disappoint several people, people who had invested heavily in him and his abilities. But he had no choice. He was forced to get this over with. And out of respect for his professor, he must do it in person.

He looked out his carriage window and recognized his surroundings. His carriage had entered London nearly an hour ago, and he identified several familiar streets and houses. He was approaching the stately home of Archibald Buchannan, one of the most esteemed surgeons in all of England. James owed Dr. Buchannan his education. He owed him for the opportunities Dr. Buchannan had given him to establish himself as one of the most promising surgeons to graduate from St. Thomas's. And he knew what Dr. Buchannan would demand in return.

James had heard the rumors that the esteemed doctor would head St. Thomas Hospital and School of Medicine, which would focus on advancements in surgery. That was what this meeting was about.

His carriage stopped in front of Dr. Buchannan's home, and James stepped out. He walked to the front entrance and was admitted by a butler then escorted into an elegant sitting room.

"James," Dr. Buchannan greeted him from across the room. "Come in, my boy. Come in."

James walked across the room and greeted his friend and mentor with a firm handshake. It was surprisingly good to see him after all this time, especially considering James knew how this meeting would conclude.

"Sit down and tell me about this quaint, backward village you've had to endure for the past year. It's quite different than the life you've known in London, I would imagine."

"Not so much," he replied. "Willowbrook has much to recommend it. It has grown over the past year at an admirable rate. New businesses are opening all the time."

"But are you the only doctor?"

"Yes, the only doctor, but there is a midwife who is remarkably skilled. She would give the students under your tutelage quite a challenge."

"*She?*" Dr. Buchannan queried in a shocked voice.

"Yes, she. She comes from several generations of midwives who are experts in using herbs to heal diseases and maladies modern medicine cannot heal. I have seen the healing power of these herbs and have to admit that they are as powerful as some of our techniques."

"Are you serious?" Dr. Buchannan asked.

"Yes, sir. I am. Under your guidance and supervision, she would be as skilled as a majority of your medical students."

"I am impressed by your recommendation, Edwards."

"That's because I have seen her tend patients and—"

James stopped mid-sentence when the door opened and Adelaide Buchannan rushed into the room.

This was the part of his time in London that he'd dreaded the most—having to confront Adelaide again and spend time with her.

"James!" she said in delight, then rushed to him and wrapped her arms around him. "I've been waiting all day for you to arrive." She turned a frowning expression on her father. "Papa, you promised to send someone to tell me the moment James arrived. I am just fortunate that I heard voices and rushed down to see who you were talking to."

"James just arrived, sweetling. I haven't even had time to offer our guest some refreshment."

"Oh," she said, reaching for a bell to summon a servant. Not long after, the door opened and the butler entered.

"Yes, Miss Buchannan?"

"Two brandies for my father and our guest, Flossen, and wine for me."

The butler poured the brandy and wine, and a maid delivered them. When she finished, the servants left the room.

"Oh, James," Adelaide said, reaching for his hand. "What have they done to you out in the middle of rural nowhere? You look like no one has bothered to feed you."

James laughed. "The citizens of Willowbrook are taking excellent care of me. And you make it sound like it is a forsaken wasteland, Adelaide. Actually, it's a beautiful area, and the people are remarkable. The town of Willowbrook is growing rapidly, due to its proximity to

London, and more people are moving in all the time."

James had been afraid Adelaide would say disparaging words about Willowbrook. According to her, anything out of London was the wilds of the earth.

"James was just telling me that he has an assistant who helps him with his patients," Dr. Buchannan said. "She is a healer."

"*She!* A healer!" Adelaide clutched her hand to her chest. "You can't be serious, James. Surely you are not associating with a healer."

"I told your father that I'm learning as much from her as she is from me."

"How can you? She is a woman!" Adelaide said, aghast. "Surely she doesn't tend to male patients. Please, tell me she does not."

"She does, Adelaide. In fact, I am only here today because of her knowledge and ability. An outbreak of typhoid went through Willowbrook, and I came down with the disease. If not for her expert care, I would not have survived."

"Well, I think I would rather be dead than have it be known that a strange woman took care of me when I was unconscious."

James was shocked to the point that he didn't know what to say. "You can't be serious, Adelaide," he said.

"Oh, I am. Completely serious."

James stared at the woman he had always known considered herself above everyone else, but this added a new degree of pomposity. As often as she had hinted that she would make him the ideal wife because of who her father was, it was more obvious than ever that she was the last person on earth he would want as partner.

He compared her to Jenny and found her completely lacking in any quality that would be worth comparing to the thoughtfulness, the compassion, the kindheartedness that Jenny possessed. Adelaide wasn't even worth comparing to Jenny. She wasn't worth sharing the same air to breathe. It was never more obvious than now.

Thankfully, Dr. Buchannan came to the rescue. "Enough talk," he interrupted. "I have made reservations for a small dinner in your honor, James, and we don't want to be late. I invited a few of the fellows you went to school with. They will enjoy seeing you after all this time."

"Oh, Father," Adelaide squealed in delight. "How brilliant of you."

"Then come now. I will show you to your room, James. You can rest for a few minutes before we will need to leave. I can't tell you how anxious everyone is to see you again. They are all eager to hear how being a doctor in the wilds of England is treating you."

James smiled. There was no other reaction to make. London doctors had lived in the city so long that they didn't understand what doctoring was truly all about. It was as if the people who lived beyond London didn't deserve to have the same medical options that the people in the upper echelons of the city were afforded.

Had it always been this way, or had he changed that much since leaving London?

LESS THAN TWO hours later, James was in the carriage with Dr. Buchannan and his daughter, on their way to the dinner his professor and mentor had organized in his honor.

The ride was extremely uncomfortable. Instead of sitting next to her father, as was appropriate for an unmarried lady, Adelaide sat beside James. Instead of keeping an acceptable amount of space between them, she sat so close to him that she was almost on his lap. Instead of her father chastising his daughter for her questionable behavior, Dr. Buchannan merely looked at James and his daughter and smiled.

James was never so relieved to arrive at their destination as he was when he could exit the carriage, enter the private dining hall, and take a drink from a passing waiter. The minute he greeted several fellow physicians with whom he'd taken classes, he was asked a barrage of questions and engaged in lively conversations.

The meal was excellent, as he knew it would be, and he took the first opportunity afforded him after the meal to join in the discussions with several groups eager to share the news that Dr. Buchannan had been given the responsibility to head a new surgical wing of St. Thomas's Hospital.

James knew what the purpose of his invitation to London was. It was to invite him to become a part of the surgical team that would head the new wing. He was honored, of course, and continued to wonder what that opportunity would mean to his career, and his future. But he would have to give up in Willowbrook, and that would never do.

He paid close attention to the discussions around him, silently letting every new justification have its own opportunity to change his mind. Even though he found the discussions interesting, he felt as though the walls were closing in around him. He invented an excuse to head toward the open terrace doors and escape the crowd, the noise… and Adelaide.

Chapter Twelve

James walked out onto the terrace to escape the barrage of questions he had been asked since entering the dinner party. Everyone wanted to know if it was as bad living in Willowbrook as they imagined it would be. They wanted to know if he regretted going to the country as much as they would if they were in his shoes. But most of all, they wanted to know why he had made the decision to go in the first place.

He'd had a posh position waiting for him in London. Dr. Buchannan had made it obvious that he wanted James to work at his side. All he had to do was go into practice with him, one of the premier surgeons in all of London, and he would be set up for the rest of his life. And, of course, eventually, he would be expected to marry Buchannan's daughter.

But that was not what he wanted.

He did not want to ride the coattails of his father-in-law. He wanted to make his own way in the world. He wanted to earn a reputation on his own.

And then he'd arrived in Willowbrook. He had met Jenny, and had fallen in love. Now he knew without a doubt that he never wanted to leave their quaint little village, or live anywhere without her.

James took a sip of his champagne and froze. He realized he was no longer alone on the terrace. He turned and faced Dr. Franklin

Rutherford, another prominent London surgeon. Although not close friends, they had gone to school together. Franklin was two years older and a brilliant surgeon. James had always been in awe of his abilities.

"I wanted to bid you a good evening, Edwards."

"You are leaving?"

"Yes. I have an early day of surgeries in the morning and must call it a night."

"Rutherford," James said, extending his hand. Franklin Rutherford had gone into practice with Buchannan, and surprisingly encouraged James not to follow in his footsteps, but to go to Willowbrook first and see if a practice in the country suited him. "I would like to thank you for the advice you offered me a year ago. You were the only physician who advised me not to jump in to practicing in London until I explored my options. I appreciate your advice."

"Does that mean you are still weighing your options?"

"No. I have made my decision. I know what I want to do."

"It sounds as if your decision isn't one Dr. Buchannan will be pleased you made."

James smiled. "Perhaps not."

"Then Dr. Buchannan won't take your decision kindly. He will definitely try to change your mind. And so will his daughter."

"I know they will, but it only took one day of visiting London to make me wish for life in Willowbrook and desire to return to the country. I can't imagine how anxious I would be to escape after a month or a year here."

"Ha!" Dr. Rutherford said. "I wish I could go back and make my decision over again."

"You would make a different choice?"

"I would definitely make a different choice."

"If ever you want to come to spend a few days in the country, don't hesitate to visit. There will always be a room waiting for you at our house."

"Our?"

James smiled broadly at the thought of having a home with Jenny at his side. "Yes. Our. By the time you come to visit, I will more than likely be married and have a home of my own."

"Good show, Edwards. I shall remember to find you should I ever manage to forsake this blasted—"

Suddenly there was a noise at the terrace doors. James caught sight of Adelaide walking across the terrace. He tried to evaluate how much of their conversation she had overheard—and hoped it wasn't much. From the wild look in her eyes, however, she had heard enough to know he had no intention of marrying her.

"Miss Adelaide," Dr. Rutherford greeted her. "I was just bidding Dr. Edwards a good evening. I have a long day of surgeries tomorrow."

"Good evening, Dr. Rutherford," Adelaide greeted him with a bubbly smile on her face that told James all he needed to know. The smile was false, as if she pretended she hadn't heard the part about Dr. Rutherford coming to visit James in Willowbrook and meeting his wife. This did not bode well.

James watched Dr. Rutherford walk across the terrace and leave the dinner. When he was out of sight, Adelaide turned back to face him.

"Papa just told me that tomorrow he is going to show you around St. Thomas's so you can see all the improvements he has planned for the school of medicine. You will also be able to observe several of the surgeries Dr. Rutherford will be performing. He is certain that watching Dr. Rutherford in action will make you want to jump right in and assist him."

"Is that what you think, too?"

"Of course, James. That is what I have always wanted. It is what I hoped you wanted for us, too."

James knew he had to set her straight now. He could not let this go on any longer. "There is no *us*, Adelaide."

"Of course there is, James. There has always been an *us*, and there still is."

James reached for her hands and held them. "No, there isn't, Adelaide. I don't care for you the same as you care for me. I am not the same person I was before I left."

"What do you mean, you are not the same person? Of course you're the same person, James. You are the man I chose to marry. The man who will step into my father's shoes when he is ready to retire. The man I will accompany to all the award celebrations, the same as I do with my father. The man who I will stand beside when they acknowledge you for your achievements and accomplishments."

"No, Adelaide. I realized long ago that this is not what I want. I don't need public accolades. I don't need to feel important."

"But *I* do. Why do you think I chose you? Why do you think I encouraged Father to mentor you and keep you under his wing? Because I knew you were going to be great someday. I knew you had the potential to be important. And *I* would be important right along with you."

James stared at her, seeing her for the person she really was. Realizing how important the accolades were for her. Realizing how important it was for her to be in the spotlight.

"But that is not what *I* want, Adelaide. I don't need to be important in anyone's eyes. I only need to help people. People who have no one else to help them. People who have no one else to turn to."

Adelaide pulled her hands from his grasp and separated herself from him. "Who changed you? Who put these ridiculous ideas into your head? Who made you think of everyone else and forget about yourself?"

"I have not forgotten about myself. I have just realized that other people are more important than I am. That people who cannot help themselves rely on me to help them. I am the only person they have."

Her eyes narrowed and the sparkle left her gaze. "Who is it? Who is *she*? Who has changed you?"

"Don't, Adelaide. It doesn't matter."

"Doesn't matter! How can you say that? She has ruined my life! She has taken you away from me!"

"I was never yours for anyone to take," he replied, but knew the second the words were out of his mouth that it was the wrong thing to say. Adelaide had always considered him hers. The entire time he was at school under her father, and her father had chosen him as his successor, she had considered him hers.

James wondered how he had been so taken in by her. He wondered why he hadn't seen what she was up to sooner, before she considered him so totally hers.

A picture of Jenny appeared in his mind. The contrast between the two was blatantly opposite. Jenny was nothing like Adelaide. Where Adelaide was controlling and selfish, Jenny was selfless. One considered everyone below herself, and the other thought of herself last.

Suddenly, James wanted to flee Adelaide's sight. He wanted to get away from her controlling, manipulating personality.

"I am going to bid your father goodnight and catch a ride home with someone. You stay and have a good night, Adelaide."

"This isn't over, James."

"I think it's best that it is, Adelaide," he said, then walked away from her.

He found her father at the front of the room and told him it had been a long day and he needed to go rest.

"Are you sure you want to leave already, James?" Dr. Buchannan asked, almost begging him to stay.

"Yes, sir. Tomorrow promises to be a busy day, and I want to be fresh for it."

"You are right, there," Dr. Buchannan said. "I can't wait to show you the progress we've made on our new surgical wing."

"And I can't wait to see it," James replied, then spied Dr. Rutherford heading for the door. "If I hurry, I think I can catch a ride with Dr. Rutherford. I'll see you in the morning, sir."

"Yes. Run along now."

"Goodnight," he said over his shoulder, then caught up with Dr. Rutherford at the door. "Would you mind dropping me off at Dr. Buchannan's home?"

"Not at all," Dr. Rutherford said with a smile. "I would have thought you would be the last one to leave, Edwards. Country life really has changed you."

James laughed. "Yes. I am much tamer now than I was a year ago."

They made it to Dr. Rutherford's carriage and headed to Buchannan's home.

"Well, has Buchannan given you the pitch for the new surgical wing at St. Thomas's?"

"Not yet," James answered. "I think he's waiting until tomorrow after I see you in action before trying to entice me to join you."

"Ah," Rutherford said. "Will his plan work?"

"No offense meant, Franklin, but I am afraid not. Nothing can convince me to return to London."

"Not even Miss Adelaide?"

James smiled. "*Especially* not Miss Adelaide. She wants someone to help her climb the social ladder, but I was never good at climbing ladders."

Rutherford released a hearty laugh. "Then you will be spared a lifetime of being manipulated."

"Yes. I will," James said, and watched the street lamps go by. These were new since he'd left, but he wouldn't miss them. He realized there was nothing about London that he would miss.

JAMES HAD BEEN gone for little more than twenty-four hours, and Jenny had been on her feet non-stop. This day had gone on forever and it was nearing dawn by the time Jenny had sent her last emergency home and cleaned up the surgery. She finished wiping everything down and put the bottles that she had used into her basket to take them home and fill them. Before she left, she heard the outer door open.

She turned, expecting to see Mrs. Copper, then remembered that she'd already left. Instead, she came face to face with one of the most beautiful women she had ever seen.

"May I help you?" Jenny asked.

"I came to talk about Dr. Edwards."

"He's not here right now. He's gone into London. Is there something I can help you with?"

"Are you a doctor?"

"No," Jenny answered. "I am Dr. Edwards's assistant. My name is Jenny Dawson."

"A pleasure to meet you, Miss Dawson. My name is Adelaide Buchannan. I am an acquaintance of James's."

"Oh, it's a pleasure to meet you, Miss Buchannan. Have you come to visit Dr. Edwards?"

The lady smiled. "Our families have been close for years. My father is one of London's most famous surgeons. Everyone thought that when James earned his degree he would go into practice with my father, but instead he decided to come out in the wilds of England and start his own practice."

"I take it that wasn't to your liking," Jenny said.

"Not at all," Miss Buchannan said. "It has put off our wedding for more than a year."

"Wedding?"

"Yes, James and I are engaged to be married. That's been a foregone assumption forever."

Jenny felt as if a rock had dropped to the pit of her stomach. James was engaged to this woman. A woman whose father could propel him to the heights that he had always dreamed of reaching.

"I see," Jenny said, reaching out to anchor herself against the nearest piece of furniture. The table was all that kept her knees from buckling beneath her.

"Do you mean James hasn't even mentioned me?" the beautiful woman asked, placing her fist on her hip in frustration. "Isn't that just like a man?"

"Yes, they often overlook the most important pieces of information."

Jenny's chest ached. She wondered if this was what it felt like for your heart to break. She wondered if her heart could go on beating if it was broken.

"Well, I must be going," Miss Buchannan said, turning toward the door. "I wish James had been here. I would have loved for him to show me around this quaint little village. I doubt that I will ever get back here again. Father is showing him around the new surgical wing he is building at St. Thomas's as we speak. He built it with James in mind. He is a remarkable surgeon, you know. Far too expert to be buried in a country village."

"Yes, he is far too good for a town like Willowbrook."

Miss Buchannan's face turned serious and her eyes took on a lethal glare. "I'm glad you understand that, Miss Dawson. I would hate for you to try to convince him that he belongs here when you know he does not. Just as I would hate for you to try to convince him that he belongs to you when he clearly does not."

Adelaide Buchannan spun away from her and left the surgery.

Jenny stared at the empty spot where Miss Buchannan had been and tried to convince herself that their conversation had all been a dream. She tried to tell herself that James wasn't engaged to someone in London, that he hadn't made love to her knowing that he was going to marry another woman, but she couldn't. He had, and yet she couldn't blame him.

He hadn't taken anything from her that she hadn't freely given him. She hadn't asked for anything in return for her body, and she hadn't intended to. She'd wanted him to make love to her. She'd wanted to know what it would be like to love him with her body the same as she did with her heart.

Now, she had to decide what she was going to do with the knowledge she had. She knew it was no longer possible to work with him, but that would not be a problem. She doubted he would even return, except to collect his equipment and personal effects, and that should only take an hour or two. She'd just make sure she was out of the office for that amount of time, then come back when he left Willowbrook.

Jenny swiped the wetness from her cheeks. She hadn't even realized she'd been crying. She didn't realize it was possible to be in such pain that the tears came unbidden. She hadn't realized it was impossible to stop them. But it was, because no matter how hard she tried, they refused to stop.

Chapter Thirteen

James was most impressed by the new surgical wing of St. Thomas's that Dr. Buchannan was building. It promised to be one of the most well-conceived structures in all of England. Perhaps in all of the medical world.

It was midday now, and his attention was riveted to what was taking place beyond the glass partition behind which he stood. He watched Franklin Rutherford perform a delicate surgery that had only been attempted a few times before, and never on British soil. James could not take his eyes off Rutherford's every move. He knew he was watching history being made.

Finally, after three hours, Dr. Rutherford finished and closed up his patient. When he was done, he replaced his instruments on the table, and they removed the patient from the operating room.

The moment the patient was out of the room, the gallery erupted in thunderous applause. Dr. Rutherford untied his surgical cap and removed it, then lifted his gaze to the onlookers in the gallery to acknowledge their applause. He was a modest man, but James could tell that even he realized that he had accomplished something monumental.

James continued to applaud until the last, then turned to face Dr. Buchannan. "Amazing," he said.

"Did that make you want to join Rutherford's team, James?"

James laughed. "Perhaps for a second, but no longer. I do not need to perform a historic procedure to feel as if I've accomplished a monumental feat. I get that same feeling when I bring a new life into the world, or save a patient who would have died had I not been there."

"Edwards, I watched you do things in the surgical theatre that I never expected to see a mere student do with such skill and confidence. You are extraordinary, man. On a par with Rutherford, here. What do I have to say, or offer you, to convince you that this is where you belong?"

"I'm afraid there's nothing you can say to entice me to leave Willowbrook."

"It is that appealing to you?"

"Yes. I love being there. I love the people, and the countryside. The medical challenges. The opportunities to innovate. I love everything about being there."

"Don't expect me to stop trying, James. You would be a perfect addition to our surgical staff."

"And I would be honored to join you, if I hadn't already found a place where I'm perfectly happy."

"Then I need to ask you, who is she?"

James smiled. "Her name is Jenny, and she stole my heart the minute I met her."

"Oh, well, I won't tell Adelaide. She has had her eyes on you since she met you."

"I know. I tried to explain about Jenny, but she didn't take the news well."

"No, I don't suppose she did. I'm afraid I've spoiled her. I've given in to her wants too much, and now she doesn't know how to take disappointment."

"Then this will be her first lesson," James said, and he was serious.

He walked out with Dr. Buchannan, and they met Dr. Rutherford coming down the hall.

"Amazing, Rutherford," James said. "I've never seen anything so magnificently done."

"Thank you, Edwards. That means a great deal coming from you. So have you decided to join us?"

James shook his head. "I am afraid not. I feel fortunate to be where I am. Now that I know what the country can offer, I don't wish to return to London."

"Keep talking, Rutherford," Dr. Buchannan said. "Maybe you can make him see sense. I have tried, to no avail. Hopefully, you will have more luck."

"I'm sorry, friends," James said. "I'm honored by your efforts, but I'll be heading back to Willowbrook in the morning."

As soon as the sentence was out of his mouth, he lifted his gaze, and his eyes locked onto the strident glare of Adelaide's hostile scowl.

"You can't be serious James," she shrieked. Her shrill voice was almost a scream. "Surely you can't mean to go back to that deplorable village."

"It's not deplorable, Adelaide."

"Of course it is. There isn't even a concert hall or a theatre."

"Buildings don't make a town, Adelaide. People do."

He watched her stride furiously toward him, her arms slicing the air about her.

"You are so blind, James. You are so infatuated by that female, you can't even see how lacking your Willowbrook is."

James stopped. "What female, Adelaide?"

"That Jenny creature."

"How do you know about Jenny? I haven't mentioned her name."

"You didn't need to. I knew someone had to have their claws into you."

James saw the jealousy in Adelaide's eyes. He saw the blind rage and the hatred. He gritted his teeth and lowered his voice, conscious of the horrid scene they were making.

"What have you done, Adelaide? How do you know about Jenny?"

"I know all about her. I knew there had to be someone holding you there, so I went to see her. She is nothing, James. Nothing!"

"So help me, Adelaide, if you did something to her—"

"That's enough, Edwards." Dr. Buchannan stepped up to his daughter and put his arm around her. "Adelaide must have heard about her somewhere."

Dr. Rutherford stepped forward. "Take your daughter home, Dr. Buchannan. I have invited James to dine with me tonight."

Adelaide's father nodded. "I think that might be for the best. Adelaide is too upset to be good company at the moment."

Dr. Buchannan escorted his fuming daughter down the hall. Adelaide turned back several times and called out to James, "You'll come back to me, James. You'll see. I am the one you want. Not her."

"Come, sweetheart," her father said, urging his daughter to go with him.

James stared after Adelaide in shock and bewilderment. He could not believe her reaction. Her blind jealousy was unnatural.

"You have never seen that side of her, have you, James?" Rutherford asked, staring after Buchannan and his daughter as they left the hospital wing.

"No. How long has she been like this?"

"Since you left. She has gradually become worse. She is so infatuated with you that she's put the two of you in a fantasy world."

"Does her father see what's going on?"

"No. Not yet. If he does, he chooses to pretend his daughter's actions are rational."

"But they're not."

"No. They are not. I have tried to talk to him, but he won't listen to me. The time will come, though, when he will have to face reality. Come with me," Rutherford said. "I've had a long day. I'm ready to go home, have a good dinner, and sit for the evening. You can stay at my house tonight. I imagine you won't want to stay at Buchannan's."

"No. If it weren't so late already, I'd head back to Willowbrook tonight."

"I know what you mean. I can see how anxious you are to return."

"If Adelaide knows about Jenny, that means she's talked to her. There's no telling what she told her."

"Nothing good, I imagine."

James agreed with his friend. He just wanted to return to Jenny and ease her mind.

He followed Rutherford from the hospital and rode with him to his home, a beautiful structure in a fashionable part of London. But James didn't care about any of that. At one point he would have, but not anymore. Not after meeting Jenny. Not after living in Willowbrook. He only wanted to get back to her and hold her in his arms and walk with her in the woods beneath the moonlight.

He only wanted to kiss her and make love to her, and tell her she was the only woman in the world for him.

He wanted to tell her he loved her and beg her to spend the rest of her life with him.

⇶⇷

HE HARDLY SLEPT at all that night, and rose before dawn. He went down the stairs, not expecting anyone to be about, but Rutherford was sitting at the breakfast table, drinking a cup of tea.

"Somehow, I knew you'd want to get an early start," he said with a smile. He poured James a cup of tea, then pushed it across the table in front of him.

"I do. I need to make sure Jenny is all right. Adelaide must have gone to Willowbrook to see her."

"Be careful of her. There is nothing she won't do to get what she wants."

James shook his head. "You don't think she'd do anything dangerous, do you?"

For a moment, Rutherford didn't answer. "I don't know. I pray not, but you never know."

James felt more anxious to leave and make sure Jenny was all right. He ate a quick breakfast, then thanked Rutherford for his hospitality and left. He had two stops to make before leaving London. He wanted to buy two gifts for Jenny, and he knew exactly what they must be.

<hr />

IT WAS MIDAFTERNOON by the time James rode into Willowbrook. Everything looked normal, but that didn't mean anything.

He went to the surgery first. Mrs. Copper sat at her desk and lifted her gaze when he entered.

"Greetings, Mrs. Copper," he said. "Is Jenny here?"

"Good afternoon, doctor. How was your trip to London?"

"Eventful. How was everything here in Willowbrook?"

"Eventful, Dr. Edwards."

"Anything I should know about?"

"You'll know soon enough," she said, then turned back to her writing.

"Is Jenny here?"

"She left for a little while."

"Will she be back?"

Mrs. Copper hesitated a moment, then breathed a heavy sigh. "I might as well tell you. You will find out soon enough."

"What is it I'll find out?"

"Miss Jenny has taken a load of her supplies home. She intends to tell you that she won't be working here once you get back."

"Are you going to tell me why?"

"Because she doesn't want to work with you once you get married and either bring your new bride back to Willowbrook, or get married and move to London."

James closed his eyes and scraped his hand over his face. "I am *not* getting married," he bellowed.

"Well, that's a relief, doctor. I understand the woman can be a bit of a—Well, it's not for me to, um, say."

"I'll be back in a bit, Mrs. Copper. Take care of anyone who comes in until I return, would you please?"

"Very well, doctor."

James left the surgery by the back door and hurried down the path to Jenny's home. Thankfully, he didn't meet her on the way, which meant she was still in her cottage.

He didn't knock when he arrived, just opened the door and went in. He found her in the bedroom unpacking some things. She lifted her gaze when she heard him enter. Her eyes were red and her cheeks were wet. She had been crying.

"Please leave, James. I don't want to talk to you."

"I know you don't. But I want to talk to you."

"I don't want to hear your excuses."

"I am not going to give you any excuses. I don't have any excuses to give you."

Another tear formed in one eye and spilled down her cheek.

"I'm not getting married to anyone but you, Jenny."

"Then you'd better tell Adelaide that, because she thinks you are marrying her."

"I've already told her. In fact, I have never asked her."

"She thinks you have."

"I know," he said on a sigh. "Adelaide is sick, Jenny. She has been in love with me since we first met. Her father was my instructor, and he took me under his wing. He was my mentor and advisor. He is the reason I came here. To get away from London, and Adelaide. He's building a new surgical wing and wanted me to come to London and work for him."

"And you refused?"

"Yes. I refused."

Jenny turned around to face him. "But that's what you've always wanted."

"It was until I came to Willowbrook and met you and the people here. This is where I want to be. You are the only one I want to be with."

"Are you sure?"

"Oh, yes, Jenny. I've never been more sure of anything in my life."

"Oh, James. I thought I'd lost you." She ran to him and wrapped her arms around his neck, then kissed him.

He returned her kiss with as much passion as he had ever given her. He kissed her again then again, each kiss filled with more emotion than the one before.

"I love you, Jenny. Don't ever doubt that I do. I couldn't live without you."

"And I could not live without you. When Adelaide told me you had asked her to marry you and I thought I had lost you, I wasn't sure I could go on."

"You will never have to live without me. I promise you that. We were meant to be together."

"Yes, we were," she replied. "You're the best root digger I've ever met. Where could I find anyone half as good as you?"

James laughed, then backed her up to the bed and came over her. He knew they shared a love that would last a lifetime. Now, he would prove it to her.

Chapter Fourteen

"I TAKE IT you patched everything up," Mrs. Copper said when they returned to the surgery.

"Yes," Jenny said, reaching for James's hand and holding it. "And look what Dr. Edwards brought back for me." She held out the stethoscope she'd draped around her neck.

"Oh, Dr. Edwards. Just what every girl wants," Mrs. Copper said on a laugh. "Their very own stethoscope."

"You are just jealous because he didn't bring one for you, aren't you?" Jenny teased.

"Oh, yes. That has always been my heart's desire. To have my very own stethoscope."

Just then, a patient entered the surgery. Millie Weaver led in two of the Claypool boys. Fred had a deep cut on his arm that would require stitches.

"What happened?" Jenny asked.

"Willie was supposed to hold the fence up so I could crawl between the wires, but he must have pulled the wire too hard and it snapped and broke, and cut my arm," Fred replied.

"Yes, it did," James said, inspecting the cut that was bleeding badly. "And what about you?" he asked the other boy. "Where are you hurt?"

"Oh, I'm not hurt," Willie said. "Millie just made me come along to watch so I'd feel sorry for him 'cause of what I'd done."

"And do you feel sorry for your brother?"

"Ya, I guess I do. But I'm happier that it happened to him than me. Fred's braver than me. He won't cry. I would have."

James laughed. "I see," he said, then took Fred to a room to work on his arm.

When they were finished, Jenny cleaned around the wound. "What should we put on the wound?" she asked James. She had a smile on her face as if she were teasing him, but she was deadly serious.

"Please hand me the jars of honey, onion, and garlic, Miss Jenny."

She handed him the jars he'd asked for, and he applied the ingredients to Fred's arm, then wrapped it in a clean bandage. "Now, I'd like the jar with anise candy in it."

Jenny gave each boy a piece of candy, then added enough that every Claypool child could have a piece. When they were all finished, they sent the boys home with Mrs. Weaver.

"Should we call it a day, Miss Dawson?" James asked.

"I think we should, Dr. Edwards. It's been a harrowing day for both of us, don't you think?"

"Yes, it has," he said, then wrapped his arm around her shoulders. They left the surgery and started walking toward Jenny's cottage. When they reached a spot out of sight of anyone, James stopped her.

"I want to talk to you, Jenny," he said.

"About what?"

"I want to ask you a question."

"All right," she said, then he led her to the stump of a tree. She sat down on the stump, and he knelt in front of her.

"I want you to know how much I love you. I love you more than I can ever explain. Will you marry me?"

James's question took her by surprise. "Are you sure?"

"I've never been more sure of anything in my life, Jenny."

Her eyes filled with tears of joy which she couldn't stop, try as she might. "I would be honored to be your wife, James. I can't think of anything I'd rather be."

James reached into his pocket and took out a small box with an elegant ring in it. He put it on her finger, then kissed her hand.

"Oh, James. It's beautiful."

"*You* are beautiful, Jenny. The most beautiful woman I have ever known. You have made me a very happy man."

She cupped his cheeks, brought his face close to hers, and kissed him. He wrapped his arms around her and gathered her to him, then lowered his head and kissed her.

"When should we marry?" she asked when they had shared several kisses.

James reached into his pocket again and pulled out a piece of paper which he handed to her. "We can marry as soon as you'd like."

Jenny unfolded the paper and read it. "It's a special license. How did you get it so soon?"

"I got it when I was in London. I had three purchases I wanted to make while I was there: your stethoscope, your ring, and a special license."

"Oh, you couldn't have done better. I love you so much."

"That's good," James said on a chuckle. "Because you're going to have to put up with me for the rest of your life."

"I can't think of anything I'd enjoy more," she said, then kissed him a final time before she let him lead her into the cottage and make love to her.

>>><<<

THEIR WEDDING WAS the biggest event the town of Willowbrook had ever seen. James and Jenny made sure there was enough reserved seating for Millie Weaver and her beau, Ralph Claypool's father, and for Mary and Ralph and their nine children, with one more on the way. The rest of the church was quickly filled until there was standing room only. Anyone who couldn't make it in when the service started was relegated to standing outside.

Mrs. Copper stood up with Jenny. As a special surprise, Edith's daughter had come from London. Jenny hadn't known Edith had a daughter, and was glad to meet her. She was nearly as old as Jenny, and she was a beautiful young lady, with auburn hair and startling green eyes.

The only person outside of Willowbrook who was issued an invitation was Dr. Rutherford, who came from London and stood up with James. Jenny had to smile when Dr. Rutherford caught his first glimpse of Mrs. Copper's daughter. It was obvious that he could not keep his eyes off her. Jenny wondered if perhaps something might come of their attraction. She hoped it would.

She and Mrs. Copper both carried bouquets of deep purple lilacs, since it was spring and they were in full bloom.

The weather was ideal and the ceremony was perfect, and before Jenny knew it, she and James were husband and wife.

The town put on a covered-dish meal to celebrate the wedding of their two doctors. James provided the drinks—gallons of lemonade and punch—and special items at their wedding feast, requested by the groom, included two dozen cakes to celebrate the occasion.

"You know everyone is going to insist that we take all the leftover cake home with us, don't you?" Jenny asked.

"I wouldn't have it any other way," James replied.

Dr. Rutherford laughed louder than anyone. "If you have cake left over, I may never leave Willowbrook until it's gone."

"That would be fine with us—wouldn't it, Jenny?"

"Absolutely!" she replied. "You're welcome to stay as long as you like. Maybe you'll take our places while we honeymoon?"

"Where are you going?" Rutherford asked.

"Nowhere," James said. "We'll just stay at Jenny's cottage and dig ginger roots. That's our favorite thing to do."

"Ginger roots?" Rutherford asked.

"Yes. You don't know what you're missing until you've dug for ginger roots. Or watched garlic dry."

Rutherford laughed a deep belly laugh. "I'd laugh even harder if I thought you weren't serious, but I know you are."

"Oh, very much so," James said, then lowered his head and kissed her. Jenny felt the nerves in her body soar. "Were you serious about filling in for me while I'm on my honeymoon?" he asked Rutherford.

"Completely," the doctor answered.

"Thank you," James replied, smiling down at Jenny. "Well, *I've* got someone to fill in for me. Who is going to fill in for you, sweetheart?"

"Well, I don't know," Jenny answered. "I guess you'll just have to have a fun honeymoon by yourself."

Everyone laughed.

"Don't worry. Mrs. Copper said she'd take over for me, and her daughter is here visiting her. She said she'd help." Jenny turned her gaze to Dr. Rutherford. "Have you met her yet?"

"No, I haven't," he answered. "I've only seen her."

"Oh, you have a treat in store. She's a beauty. I'm just glad Mrs. Copper will help and thought to bring her daughter in, as well."

"Oh, I love that lady," James said, wrapping his arms around Jenny's shoulders and squeezing her.

"We haven't even been married an hour and he's already in love with someone else," she teased.

"Don't worry, Jenny," Rutherford said. "I'll be waiting on the sidelines if you ever get tired of your husband."

"Did you hear that, sweetheart?" she said, cupping James's cheek and pulling his head down for a kiss.

"Find your own girl, Franklin. This one is mine."

Everyone laughed at their good-natured teasing.

"Come on," Jenny said to James. "Let's greet our guests and get something to eat." She pointed to a table filled with cakes. "You have a lot of cake to demolish."

"Oh, lead me to the largest piece of chocolate cake right now. I can't wait to—"

"No!"

James's vision locked on the figure frozen behind Jenny.

Adelaide stood with a gun pointed at his wife. It was clear that she intended to shoot her.

"Jenny! Move!"

Everything moved in slow motion from that point.

Adelaide Buchannan lifted the gun and pointed it at Jenny's chest.

The moment Jenny saw her, she began to turn away, but the gun fired, and a bullet hit her.

"Jenny!"

Thankfully, several men standing close to Adelaide grabbed her and subdued her. They took away her gun and pointed it at her.

Her gaze locked with Jenny's, and James stared at the female who had ruined his day and possibly his life. Her eyes were filled with bitter hatred as vile as anything he had ever seen.

"I hope you die, you bitch. You can't have him. He's mine." Adelaide struggled to free herself from the arms that held her. "He's mine!"

"Jenny," James said, lifting his wife into his arms. He pressed his hand against the wet spot on her dress.

"Get her to the surgery," Rutherford commanded, helping James to his feet.

"Stay with me, Jenny," James begged. He knew she was hurt badly enough that she could die. "Stay with me, sweetheart."

"It's all right, James," she said. "It doesn't even hurt."

"That's good," he said, but the expression in Rutherford's eyes told him that it wasn't good. It told him Jenny was going into shock. It told him everything he already knew but didn't want to admit. It told him he was losing her. "Stay with me, Jenny. Don't you leave me."

"I'm going to scrub," Rutherford said when they reached the surgery. "You wash Jenny."

"Would you do it?" James asked. "I'm not sure I can."

"Yes, I'll do it. You can assist me."

James nodded.

Suddenly, the door opened and Mrs. Copper entered. She didn't say anything, just stood against the wall and watched. Every once in a while she walked out and gave the growing crowd an update, then she came back in and watched.

"Talk to her, James," Rutherford told him. "Don't let her leave us."

James leaned close to his wife and whispered in her ear. "Don't you leave me, Jenny. Don't you dare leave me. I can't survive without you. I can't. I don't want to go on without you."

Over and over he said the same words to her. Over and over he told her how much he loved her and how he couldn't live without her, while at the same time he watched every move Rutherford made.

The doctor's hands were calm and steady. His movements were quick and accurate. It wasn't long before James heard the clink of a metal bullet hitting a pan.

"Got it," Rutherford said. "She's lucky. The bullet missed her heart."

James said a silent thank you to God. They were almost done. It wouldn't be long now and Rutherford would close her up. Then they would just have to watch for infection and a fever.

James went to a cabinet in Jenny's room and brought back the jars she'd told him to use on wounds: a jar of honey, ground turmeric, ground garlic, and several other spices.

"What do I do with this?" Rutherford asked when James handed him the jar of honey.

"Put it on the wound."

Rutherford looked at him skeptically.

"It works, Frank. I've seen it."

Rutherford didn't question him further—he applied honey to the wound.

The doctors continued to work on Jenny. When they finished, they placed a bandage that extended from her chest up across her shoulder.

James took her hand in his and squeezed her fingers. There was no response, but she was still breathing. That was all James cared about. She was still alive.

Chapter Fifteen

Everything that had happened to Jenny was his fault. James knew that without a doubt. If he had been firmer with Adelaide when he realized what a fantasy world she had created with him, this wouldn't have happened. But even in his wildest imagination, he hadn't realized how demented she'd become. He hadn't realized how dangerous she was to anyone who threatened her fantasy future with him.

"James?" Rutherford whispered a short while after the sun had come up. At least Jenny had survived the first night. "Dr. Buchannan is here. He would like to speak to you. Go on. I will sit with her."

James looked at Jenny, and tears filled his eyes. He tried to be strong, but he was still terrified he would lose her.

"Don't let her die while I'm gone," he said, even though he knew Rutherford had no control over that.

"I won't, James. She is not going to die."

James nodded, then rose and walked out the door.

Buchannan stood on the other side of the room and watched out the window. "Have you seen how many people are here?"

James shook his head then walked to the window and looked out. At least half the town appeared to be waiting to hear word of Jenny's progress.

"She must be very well liked," Buchannan said.

"She is," James replied. "She is loved by the entire town."

"I don't know what to say," Buchannan said.

"There's nothing you can say." James turned and glared at the man who had been his teacher and his mentor. "The question is, what are you going to do?"

"What am *I* going to do?" Buchannan seemed surprised by the question. "What do you mean, what am I going to do?"

"I mean, what are you going to do with your daughter? She has a problem, and yesterday was only the first time she'll try to kill Jenny. If you do not lock her up, she'll attempt to kill her again, and next time she might succeed."

"What are you saying, Edwards?"

James took a threatening step forward and locked his hostile glare with Buchannan's. "I am saying that your daughter is mentally unstable," he said with barely controlled anger. "Anyone who attempts to kill another human being is unstable."

"No," Buchannan said, shaking his head.

"Yes! And you need to face it, Buchannan! You can either take her to a sanatorium where she can be locked away and not come after Jenny again, or I will press charges and she will go to trial. I guarantee you if she's found guilty of attempted murder, she'll go to prison, and her life will be much worse there than in a private sanatorium. The choice is yours. I promise you, all those people out there will testify that she attempted to kill my wife."

Buchannan's face lost its color. His shoulders slumped and he aged several years in a matter of seconds. "What happened to her?" he asked, as if he was desperate to find the answer to a question that puzzled him.

"You spoiled her is what happened. You provided everything she wanted until she thought she deserved whatever she desired, and when she didn't get something she wanted, she thought she had the right to eliminate whoever prevented her from getting it."

Buchannan released a heavy sigh. "I will take care of her."

"No!" James bellowed. "You will not *take care* of her. You will have her incarcerated in a heavily guarded detention complex with no chance of escape. You will have her confined indefinitely, and I will be notified any time she is permitted to leave the complex. Is that understood?"

Dr. Buchannan trembled in fear. He knew how close James was to having Adelaide charged with attempted murder and how close she was to being thrown into prison for the rest of her life.

"Y-yes," he stammered.

"You are fortunate my wife is still alive. You'd better hope she stays alive. If she dies, I will see that your daughter hangs for murder."

"James, what am I going to do?"

"You are going to do what I said. You are going to have her incarcerated. You will make sure she never sees the light of day again!"

Buchannan stared at James with a look of disbelief, then gave him a short nod. With shoulders still slumped, he turned and left the room.

James closed his eyes and tried to calm his nerves. He had never been so furious in his life. Never been so frightened.

He took a deep breath and returned to the room where Jenny lay. He needed to see her and be with her. He needed to sit with her and hold her hand. He needed to share with her all the strength he had so she did not die, but kept breathing.

"I think you put the fear of God in Buchannan," Rutherford said, patting James on the shoulder.

"I meant every word I said, Franklin. So help me, if Jenny dies, I'll hunt Adelaide down and kill her myself."

"You won't have to, James. Jenny won't die. We won't let her."

James looked at his friend and nodded in agreement, then he checked his wife to make sure she hadn't developed a fever.

"Get some rest now," he said, and showed Rutherford to a room with a bed. "I'll sit with Jenny. I have a lot to tell her."

Now the waiting would begin. Now the long, endless hours of watching her to make sure she was still breathing would start. And the never-ending hours of checking to make sure she hadn't developed a fever.

While he watched her, he relived the times he had accompanied Jenny to her garden and dug roots and picked berries and tied garlic bulbs together and hung them to dry. He relived the nights they had lain beneath the stars and made love.

He reached for her hand and held it. He would never forget those nights. He would never forget any of the times he had spent with her. They were the most special nights of his life.

The sun was lowering in the sky when there was a soft knock on the door and Mrs. Copper entered. Her daughter followed her into the room.

"How is she?" Mrs. Copper asked with a concerned look on her face.

"Still asleep," James answered.

"I brought you some dinner. Even though I was sure you weren't hungry, it's important that you eat. You need to keep up your strength."

"No, I'm not. But perhaps Franklin will be when he wakes."

"He can eat something if he is. And there's plenty of cake in the front room. Everyone insisted on leaving their cakes for you."

James forced a smile to his face. He wasn't sure he could eat a piece of cake. Those were his wedding cakes. A wedding that had ended in disaster.

"I saw Dr. Buchannan leave a bit ago," she said.

"Yes. I told him to lock his daughter away where she can never harm anyone else, or I'm not sure what I'll do."

"If you don't, there are several citizens of Willowbrook who will. Miss Jenny is loved in this town. She's delivered nearly all the children in Willowbrook for the last ten years and more."

James lowered his gaze to where Jenny lay on the bed. She was sleeping, but her slumber was not restful. It was agitated, as if she struggled to fight the pain.

"How is she doing?" Rutherford said, coming in from the other room.

"No fever, so far," James said, feeling her forehead again. He rinsed a cloth in cool water and placed it on her neck.

"Don't tell me you think it was the honey," Rutherford said. He wore a smile on his face.

"No, I won't tell you I think it was the honey," James answered. "I *know* it was. Don't ask me how I know it, but I've seen it work."

"Why don't we know about this in London, then?"

"What do you think Buchannan and all the other surgeons would say if you told them to make sure they used honey on wounds to avoid infection? And onions and garlic and oregano?"

"They'd laugh you right out of the operating room."

"That's right. That's medieval medicine. It's witchcraft."

"Is that how you felt about it when Jenny first told you about it?"

"Of course. The first patient I saw her use it on was an appendicitis patient. I saw him heal in record time."

James placed his hand on Jenny's forehead again and breathed a sigh of relief when her skin was not overly warm. Then he reached for her hand and held it. She squeezed his fingers. At least, he thought she did. Or maybe it was wishful thinking.

"Have you met my daughter, Dr. Rutherford?" Mrs. Copper said.

"No, Mrs. Copper. I haven't had the pleasure," Rutherford replied.

"Winnie, I'd like to introduce you to Dr. Franklin Rutherford. Dr. Rutherford, this is my daughter, Winnifred Copper."

"It's a pleasure to meet you," Rutherford said, reaching for Winnie's hand.

James noticed the expression in his friend's gaze when he looked at Winnie Copper. He couldn't wait to tell Jenny. It was the same look he had seen in Jenny's eyes when she looked at him. The same look he knew he'd had in his own eye when he looked at her.

"There's some food in the front room," Mrs. Copper told Rutherford. "And a dozen or more cakes. No one wanted to take their cake home. They left them for the two of you to eat. Winnie will help you dish up two plates."

Rutherford laughed then followed Winnie toward the front room to get a plate of food.

"I'll bring you a little bit to eat, Dr. Edwards," Winnie said. "I know you're not hungry, but you have to eat a little something."

"Yes," Rutherford said. "I doubt James has eaten all day."

James knew better than to argue. He knew his friend well enough to know he would bring him a plate of food whether he wanted one or not.

Rutherford and Winnie were gone several minutes, and when they returned, they had several sandwiches on a plate for James, and she was carrying several pieces of cake for them to eat later.

"Look at that," Mrs. Copper said, pointing at the cake. "And you let him operate on Jenny. He massacred cutting the cake."

James knew they were trying to add a little humor into the situation, and even though he didn't feel like laughing, he couldn't help himself. Rutherford *had* massacred the cake.

They sat with Jenny a while longer, then Mrs. Copper and Winnie went home for the night, promising they'd return tomorrow. Rutherford finished his dinner, then poured them each a glass of brandy. James was glad for it.

He watched Jenny and tried to convince himself that she looked better. Tried to convince himself that she was getting better. But he knew it was too early for her to improve. At least she hadn't developed a fever yet. Hopefully, she wouldn't. Hopefully, her honey would work like he knew it could.

James sat beside Jenny's bed all night. He held her hand and rubbed circles on the top of her hand.

"Have you slept at all?" Rutherford asked when he rose the next morning.

"I might have," James answered.

"That means you haven't. Is Mrs. Copper here yet?"

"Yes, she got here about an hour ago."

"Did her daughter come with her?"

"No, she came alone, but she said Winnie would come later."

"Oh."

"Disappointed?" James asked.

"No. I just wondered about Mrs. Copper. If she was here, that means she's made coffee and tea. Which one do you want?"

"Coffee," James answered.

"You know I am going to steal her away from you, don't you? She makes the best coffee in Britain."

"Her tea isn't bad, either," James said. "But you're wasting your time if you think you can steal her away from us."

"Why? Do you think she likes you that much?"

James shook his head. "Not me. Jenny. She would never leave Jenny."

"You married quite a lady, James."

"Yes, I did. Everyone in town loves her."

"That is obvious. You still have a crowd of townspeople standing in front of your surgery waiting for word on Jenny's condition."

James glanced out the window. "Would you go talk to them?"

"What do you want me to say?"

"Just tell them she is still asleep and we'll let them know when she wakes. Take Mrs. Copper with you. She will know what to say."

When Rutherford and Mrs. Copper went outside, James turned back to Jenny and reached for her hand. He held it for a long time, then leaned in and kissed her cheek.

"I love you, Jenny. You have to get better. You can't die on me," he said as the first tears streamed down his cheeks. "I'm trying so hard to be strong, but I'm failing. I could never survive without you. I could never live another day if you weren't in my world."

He swiped the tears from his eyes then leaned in and kissed her again. "I should have watched her closer. I should have realized what a danger Adelaide was, what she was capable of. But I didn't. It's all my fault."

He brushed Jenny's hair from her face and straightened her covers. He simply wanted her to get better. He just wanted this part of the healing process to be over. He wanted to know that she would be all right. Wanted her awake so she could tell him she was going to live.

"I love you, sweetheart. I didn't tell you that I loved you enough. I didn't tell you how much you mean to me, but you mean the world to me."

Before he could say more, the door opened and Rutherford and Mrs. Copper returned. "You have to get better, Jenny," Mrs. Copper whispered in her ear. "You are causing the whole town of Willowbrook a great deal of worry. Even little Harry Claypool is crying in his mama's skirt. Of course, I think it's because he doesn't think he'll get any more anise candy, but nevertheless, he's extremely sad."

There was a knock on the door, and Winnie entered the room followed by two men from the restaurant. They both carried plates of food. "Mrs. Chester said you had to eat something before you waste away," the taller of the two men said.

"Tell Mrs. Chester thank you," Mrs. Copper said, then rose to go to the front room. "Winnie, come help me fix two plates of food, but I told Mrs. Chester she didn't have to send any desserts. We have enough cake to last until next Christmas."

James tried to smile. "Franklin, go out in the front room and eat with Winnie and Mrs. Copper. Just put a little food on a plate for me. I'll eat in here with Jenny."

Rutherford left and returned with some food, then James sat with

Jenny and slid the food around on his plate. He wasn't hungry. How could he be when his wife was so close to dying?

He put his plate down on the table beside the bed and reached for her hand again. He leaned over and kissed her cheek. He loved her so much. "Don't you leave me, Jenny. Do you hear me? You can't leave me. I don't want to live without you. I'm not sure I can survive without you."

He held her hand and placed his head on the bed beside her and closed his eyes. There was nothing left to do but pray that she would survive. Her life was in God's hands now.

Chapter Sixteen

James must have fallen into a deep sleep. He wasn't sure what he was dreaming, but he was sure something was crawling on his skin. He brushed it away, but it didn't stop. It moved again.

He brushed at it again, then woke with a start. There was nothing crawling on his skin. It was Jenny moving ever so slowly as she struggled to wake.

"Jenny!" he whispered. "Jenny, sweetheart. Are you waking?"

She turned her head and tried to open her eyes.

It was morning. The sun was just peeking over the horizon.

"Jenny? Sweetheart? Franklin!" he called out, and Rutherford entered the room. "She's waking. I'm sure she's trying to waken."

Rutherford felt her forehead, then her cheeks. He lifted the cover on her shoulder and felt her skin there, then lifted the bandage. "She's warm, James. But there's no infection."

James smiled. "Of course not. We put honey on her wound."

Rutherford rolled his eyes and smiled. "Do you really believe that honey works?"

"Of course I do. And after you've seen it work time after time, you will, too."

James took her hand, brought her fingers to his lips, and kissed her. She turned her head from side to side.

"Don't hurry, Jenny. You can wake whenever you're ready.

There's no hurry."

She moaned.

"Would you like something to drink?" he said, reaching for a glass of water. She opened her mouth a small slit, and he held a spoonful of water to her lips. She didn't take much, but it was more than she'd had for the last two days.

Her eyes didn't open, but she tried. James had never been so happy in his life.

Rutherford put a fresh bandage across her chest and shoulder—at James's insistence, applying more honey. Before they were done caring for Jenny, she'd fallen asleep again. But she had taken a step in the right direction. Perhaps she was on the road to recovery. He prayed she was.

"Do you think she is recovering?" Winnie Copper asked later that afternoon when she brought in fresh coffee.

"I do," James answered.

She looked at Rutherford and waited for his response. "Yes, she is. She's much better than she was yesterday."

"Good—I'll tell Mother to share the news with the people who are waiting outside. They will be ever so relieved."

Rutherford took a sip of coffee, then asked, "Did you make this?"

James saw Winnie smile as she nodded.

"Your coffee is as good as your mama's, and that is a high compliment," Rutherford said.

"She taught me, so I am sure it is."

"Franklin, go out with Winnie and Mrs. Copper and tell the people that Jenny is trying to wake," James said.

Rutherford nodded, then followed Winnie from the room.

James couldn't wait to tell Jenny of the budding romance between his friend and Winnie. She would be so pleased. She had told him there was nothing she enjoyed more than watching two people fall in love.

JENNY SLEPT OFF and on for the next few days. She was never completely awake or aware of her surroundings, but at least she knew where she was. On the third day after she had opened her eyes that first time, she opened them for good.

"Well, Jenny," James said. "Welcome back."

"James?" she croaked.

"Don't talk, Mrs. Edwards. I'll do the talking."

"What happened?" she muttered.

"Adelaide shot you. I guess she was really angry that I married you instead of her."

"Where…?"

"She's locked up where she can't hurt anyone ever again."

Jenny nodded.

"I want you to listen to something, sweetheart." James went to the window and opened it wide. He leaned out and yelled, "She's awake!"

The thunderous cheers were deafening.

"Those are the people of Willowbrook. They've been keeping vigil outside the surgery all this time."

Jenny's eyes filled with tears that spilled down her cheeks.

"You are well loved, sweetheart. Don't ever forget it."

Just then, Rutherford, Winnie, and Mrs. Copper ran into the room. "We heard that rousing cheer. Does that mean Jenny's awake?" Mrs. Copper asked.

"That's exactly what it means. She's awake, probably not for long, but at least for a while."

James gave her more water to drink, then held a glass of laudanum-laced wine to her lips, and she drank that. He knew that would make her go to sleep again, but that wasn't a bad thing. She needed to sleep.

※※※※

JENNY COULDN'T REMEMBER sleeping so much in her life. She'd wake for a little while and go back to sleep. For some reason, she was exhausted. She blamed it on the medicine James gave her. She was sure there was laudanum in the wine.

She opened her eyes when the door opened, and smiled at James walking toward her. "You can stop giving me whatever it is that's in the wine, James. All it does is make me sleep."

"Very well, sweetheart," he said, before stepping over to the bed and leaning down to kiss her. "But it isn't only making you sleep. It's also keeping the pain away."

"Then you need to give me some feverfew tea, or willow bark tea. That will take away the pain without making me sleep all the time."

He smiled at her, then reached for her hand. "How would you like to get out of bed for a while?"

"Oh, yes! There's nothing I'd like more."

James threw back the covers, then reached for Jenny's robe and slipped it around her shoulders.

"Can I go outside for a bit?"

"Perhaps," he said. "Maybe as far as the park. But not for long."

"Oh, yes," she said excitedly.

James slipped a cloak around her so she was adequately covered, then took her out the surgery door and across the street to the park. Jenny hoped that they could make it all the way to the first bench in the park before anyone noticed her, but they weren't so lucky.

"Oh, Jenny!" the first voice greeted her from a lane in the park.

Before she could get settled on the bench, a crowd had gathered around her.

James let them pummel her with questions for a little while, then interrupted the well-wishers and explained that it was time for Jenny to return to bed.

"Oh, how exciting," she said on their way back to the surgery.

"See if I let you out in public again. You caused a bigger crowd than the queen coming to visit."

"It was exciting, wasn't it?"

He lowered his gaze and smiled at her. "Yes, it was. I'm just so happy that you are so much better. I was so afraid I was going to lose you."

She leaned her head on his shoulder. "I was afraid you might, too, and I didn't want to leave you."

James took her back into the surgery and put her back to bed. He didn't want to think how he would survive if she had left him. Jenny had become his whole life.

EACH DAY SHE got better, until the day came when she was healed enough to return home.

"How much longer can you stay, Franklin?" James asked when he was ready to escort Jenny home. "My wife and I would like to take our honeymoon, now."

"It's about time!" Rutherford said. "I've heard stories about wives that were so nervous about their wedding nights that they thought of excuses to put them off. But I've never heard of a wife getting shot to postpone her wedding night."

"Very funny," James said on a laugh.

"I had something I wanted to talk over with you and Jenny, but the time wasn't quite right before. But now I think it is."

"What?"

"I had a patient yesterday," Rutherford said. "At least, I thought he was a patient when he first came in, but when I was alone with him, he told me he was the mayor of the small town just beyond Willowbrook."

"Cedar Ridge?"

"Yes. Cedar Ridge is in need of a doctor. He asked me if I would consider accepting his offer to start a practice there."

"Oh, Franklin," Jenny said. "Cedar Ridge is a wonderful village. It got its start very similarly to Willowbrook. It's still in its infant stage, but in a few years, it will grow the same as Willowbrook has."

"That's what the mayor thinks."

"Are you really considering leaving London?" James asked.

Rutherford shrugged. "I don't know. Would I consider giving up a life in London that we both hated for a life like the one you love here in the country? I think I would. In fact, I know I would."

"Have you talked this over with Winnie?" James asked.

Rutherford's cheeks darkened. "She thinks it would be a good idea."

"Oh, wonderful," Jenny squealed.

Both men laughed.

"For a while, you could help me out here in Willowbrook a day or two a week," James said. "At least until Jenny is well enough to come back."

"That would be ideal," Rutherford said. "I want to think it over a day or two longer before I make a decision."

"That sounds like a wise plan," Jenny said. "It will be good to have you close, Franklin."

"Thank you. Nothing is written in stone, but I think I might be ready to make a move."

"Well, in the meantime, I still want to have a honeymoon with my wife," James said. "Can I count on you to stay here long enough for my wife and I to have some time alone before we're thrust back to work?"

"You can," Rutherford answered. "It would be my pleasure."

"Are you ready to go home, Jenny, and see if your cottage is still standing?"

"I've been ready for more than a month," Jenny said, then she and James got ready.

When the time came that they traveled back home, James made sure they moved slowly enough that Jenny didn't overdo it.

He opened the door, then lifted Jenny in his arms and carried her into the house.

"Oh, I've missed it here," Jenny said, looking around at all the herbs and bulbs still where she'd left them. She turned to look at James, then cupped his cheek. "Do you know how much I love you?"

"I think so, sweetheart, but I wouldn't mind if you reminded me," he answered.

"I love you more than the sun, the moon, and the stars."

"And I love you more than heaven and the earth," James replied.

And James took her to their bedroom and made love to her until the moon chased away the sun, and the stars twinkled from above.

Epilogue

JAMES WALKED THE familiar path to the cottage he shared with Jenny. His thoughts turned from the day nearly three years ago when he'd married her to all the events that had happened since.

The most traumatic of those events was their wedding day, when Adelaide Buchannan had shot Jenny in an attempt to kill her, and she'd almost succeeded. Thankfully, though, Jenny had survived, thanks to the help and skill of Franklin Rutherford, who had removed the bullet still in her flesh and saved her, and her husband who insisted upon using Jenny's proven herbal wound care.

Since then, Rutherford had started his own surgery in nearby Cedar Ridge. He'd worked there three days a week, and at James's surgery three days a week, until his practice developed a large enough client list. As his patient list increased, so did the days of the week he spent in Cedar Ridge, until he had informed James that he needed to work full time at his own surgery.

James had known that day would come, but the Willowbrook surgery had grown so much that he wasn't sure how he could get along without Rutherford. They'd grown closer as friends over the years they'd worked together. Instead of losing Rutherford, he offered him a partnership in the Willowbrook surgery. James gave him enough time to find a replacement for the Cedar Ridge practice, and when he had someone to take his place, Rutherford would work full time in Willowbrook.

The second monumental event that had occurred over the last three years was the birth of his and Jenny's first child, a daughter, Alice Ann. James always knew he looked forward to being a father, but he had no idea how special that having a child of his own would be until little Ali was born. Then, two years later, he was blessed with the birth of his second child—a son, Frank, named after his good friend Franklin Rutherford.

Baby Frank was six months old now and growing like a weed. It was a miracle how special James's family was. He couldn't possibly love them any more than he did.

James opened the cottage door and stepped inside. Jenny had both children on her lap. She was feeding the baby and rocking a sleeping Ali.

"If this isn't a perfect picture, I don't know what is," James whispered. He leaned over Jenny and kissed her on the cheek.

"You're home early. Is something wrong?"

"Yes, and no."

"That's a vague answer," she said. "Why don't you take Ali and put her in her bed, and I'll put the baby in his cot."

James gathered Ali and carried her to her bed, while Jenny carried the baby to his cot. Luckily, they both stayed asleep while he and Jenny crept from the room.

Instead of staying in the cottage, they left by the kitchen door and sat on the step where they could hear the children if they woke up.

"Very well, James. What is it?"

He wrapped his arm around Jenny's shoulders. "Actually, there is quite a bit."

"Well, then, perhaps you should start with the most important thing first."

"That sounds like a good plan," he said with a smile. "Do you know that house we've been looking at?"

"The one we said we'd love to have if it ever came up for sale?"

"Yes, that one. Well, it's for sale."

"Is it?" Jenny asked with an excited look on her face.

"Yes. Old man Jeffers is moving to Cedar Ridge to live with his son and his family. He said the house was just too big for him now that his wife is gone, and his son wants him to move closer."

"Do you know how much it will cost us? Can we afford it?"

"I hope so, because I bought it this morning."

"Oh, James!" Jenny wrapped her arms around his neck and kissed him. "Did you really?"

"Yes. I really did."

"I'm so glad," Jenny said, "because I'm not sure yet, but I think I may be adding to our family."

"Really?"

"Yes."

"Then it's a good thing I bought the house. You're already filling it up as fast as Mary Claypool filled up her house."

"Yes, but at least I think she may be done having babies. At least, she hasn't had any more since the last one three years ago."

"She doesn't need to. You've taken over for her."

"I don't get pregnant by myself, you know."

"I know full well," he replied, then leaned over and kissed her tenderly.

"And the next bit of news?"

"I just offered Franklin a partnership in the surgery."

James watched the expression on Jenny's face to see her reaction. Thankfully, it was one of approval.

"Does that meet with your approval?"

"Oh, yes. Yes!" she answered. "I wondered how I was going to tell you that I wanted to be a full-time mother to our children. And I know that Winnie wants to be a full-time mother to their children. We both loved working with you and Franklin before the children were born, but now they are our first responsibilities. We want to be full-time mothers to them."

"Then that's what you will be, because you were born to be a mother."

"And you are a perfect father. Our children couldn't ask for a more kind and loving parent."

He leaned over and kissed Jenny again. This time his kisses were filled with all the passion and desire he felt for her.

She answered his kisses with just as much passion, then lifted her lips from his to stop his kisses before they turned into more than just kisses.

"Was that all your news?" she asked breathlessly.

"No. There is one more bit of news I received today. But it is not as happy."

"What is it, James?"

James reached into his pocket and removed a letter, then handed it to her.

Jenny unfolded it, then slowly read the words. It wasn't long, and her eyes filled with tears. She finished the letter, then looked up at him, letting the tears run down her cheeks.

"She's dead," Jenny whispered. "Adelaide killed herself. Oh, she was such a tortured woman."

"Yes, and I feel like it was partly my fault."

"It was not your fault, James. It was no one's fault. She was just so used to getting whatever she wanted that when she wanted something she couldn't have, she didn't know how to handle the rejection."

"That may be true, but it doesn't make it any easier to live with."

"Perhaps not, but it's a lesson we can all learn from. Especially with our children. There will be disappointments in life that they will have to deal with. And we will be with them to help them through those difficult times."

James wrapped his arm around Jenny's shoulder and brought her closer to him. She nestled her head beneath his chin and breathed a deep sigh.

"I love you, Jenny," he whispered.

"And I love you, James. Never forget that we were made for each other. Forever and always."

About the Author

Laura Landon taught high school for ten years before leaving the classroom to open her own ice-cream shop. As much as she loved serving up sundaes and malts from behind the counter, she closed up shop after penning her first novel. Now she spends nearly every waking minute writing, guiding her heroes and heroines to find their happily ever afters.

She is the author of more than a dozen historical novels, including SILENT REVENGE, INTIMATE DECEPTION, and her newest Montlake Romance release, INTIMATE SURRENDER.

Her books are enjoyed by readers around the world.

Made in United States
Orlando, FL
01 November 2023